HE HAD IT COMING

Also by Camika Spencer

Cubicles

When All Hell Breaks Loose

HE HAD
IT COMING

CAMIKA SPENCER

ST. MARTIN'S PRESS ✹ NEW YORK

ISBN 0-312-32334-4

To Page Turners Book Club of Dallas

LaShawnda
Charlene
Kris
Angie
Sharon
Etta
Arnetria

Always hooking up for a good read!

ACKNOWLEDGMENTS

GRATITUDE AND APPRECIATION go to God, the universe, my family, the St. Martin's family, friends, supporters, and fans. We all just keep getting better. Extra love goes out to the copy editors of this book. May God continue to bless your silent frustrations and general angst when it comes to dealing with authors like me. Finally, to Matt Bialer and Jennifer Enderlin: Thank you for your faith, honesty, energy, guidance, and for being damn good at what you do. You see greatness in potential. May all our endeavors continue to be fruitful and allow us to sleep at night knowing our work has not been in vain. Be cool.

HE HAD IT COMING

MARCUS BROOKS WOKE UP naked and hungover. His head throbbed, his mouth was cotton-dry, and he could barely get out of bed. It was six thirty, and the sun peeked over the Atlanta skyline. His room, an open space with clothes, wineglasses, and ashtrays strewn about the floor, was still shaded by the cascading deep blue-blackness of the coming morning.

Marcus stretched and yawned so loud, his presence filled the room. Now that he was awake, he could take control of his day. First, he greeted his mother, who stood square-shouldered in a framed, four-by-six photo on the nightstand next to his bed.

"Good morning, beautiful," he said.

Junesta Brooks was a stout woman with a proud face, sturdy build, and dark features. Marcus inherited her short but wide nose, smoldering eyes, unibrow, and rich brown skin tone. Junesta had been dead for twelve years, but Marcus kept her memory alive by taking her picture with him no matter where he went. But today they were home.

He kissed the photo and put it back in its place.

Marcus took a whiff of his armpits and of the air around him. The scent of the three P's infiltrated his nose: pussy, perfume, and perspiration. He needed to take a shower, but first, he needed to get rid of the strange woman asleep in his bed.

He walked around to get a glimpse of the woman's face. The truth was, he didn't know her and couldn't remember her name, where she'd come from, or how she'd ended up in his apartment. Her cinnamon-colored skin revealed a rose tattoo that was etched onto her shoulder, and her hair was the color of copper—still, none of those details called up her name. She snored lightly, unaware that Marcus was standing over her. The empty bottle of Crown whiskey on his floor along with cigarette butts, empty condom wrappers, and weed roaches were the evidence of a hard night of socializing and sex. Whoever she was, she knew how to have a good time, but like all the other one-night stands in his life, she had an appointment with the front door. Marcus had a strict twelve-hour rule for female company, and she was an hour away from being in violation.

Marcus grabbed the woman by her feet and pulled her down from the head of the bed. "Hey, wake up."

She wiggled her feet free of his tugging and moaned in protest without opening her eyes. She was going to be a challenge, and he wasn't in the mood.

Marcus tried again. This time he jerked the sheets from her body. "You need to get your ass up," he said. "This ain't the Embassy fucking Suites."

She cracked open an eye long enough to take a peek at the red digital numbers on the clock; then she curled into a fetal position and let her eye close. "It's still early." Her voice was groggy but pleasant. She patted the mattress. "Don't you want to come back to bed, Mr. Brooks?"

Most of his fans called him Mr. Brooks, so at least he knew that much; this woman was probably one of the many lusting groupies who waited outside his high-rise building just to get the opportunity to sleep with him.

"No." Marcus wasn't moved by her passivity. He wanted her out. He removed a bra from the lampshade and tossed it on the bed. "It's time for you to go."

"What's your problem?" Her voice became deep, reedy, and without pretense.

"I don't have a problem."

"Then what's your rush?" She grabbed a pillow and hoisted herself comfortably against it, giving him a clearer view of her rounded shoulders, slab thighs, love handles, and busty upper body. The few attractive features included her pouty lips and full but girlish face. She definitely was no Janet Jackson, but last night he probably couldn't tell. In the dark, drunk and high, it all felt the same.

"No rush. I just want you out of my house."

"Why?"

"Because it's time for you to go."

The woman scratched her head and yawned without adding any quickness to her actions. "I'll need a ride back to my hotel."

"You can catch a cab."

"Can you call me one?"

"I can give you the phone book."

"I guess chivalry is dead," she said. Her comment seemed more of an afterthought. She turned her back to Marcus. Now he had to look at her ass. Unlike asses he was used to, this ass was invaded by cellulite dimples and stretch marks.

Marcus yawned and scratched his testicles.

The woman fell back onto the pillow. "Can I at least let the tequila shots and weed wear off? I'm dead tired, you know."

"I don't let any bitch recuperate in my bed. I have a twelve-hour-stay rule, and you are in violation."

His words made her sit up again. "I don't give a damn about your rule, and who are you calling a bitch?"

"Don't act offended," Marcus said. "Women call each other bitches all the time." He grabbed two empty condom packets from the floor and tossed them in a wastebasket. "I'm just calling it like I see it—don't take it personal."

It was the trigger she needed. Without another word, the woman moved to the edge of the bed and began searching for her clothes.

He noticed the necklace she wore. Dangling from the chain was a diamond-encrusted letter *S*.

Stacy? Marcus thought. No. She didn't look like a Stacy. From the middle-aged weight her face carried along with the strands of gray in her hair, she looked more like a Sandra or Sylvia. For all he knew, the letter could stand for her last name and not her first. He decided it wasn't important. Once she was gone, she would be gone.

"For the record," she said between strapping her feet into her high heels. "I'm not a bitch, and if you call me that again, you *will* regret it."

"Don't threaten me." Marcus responded with ice in his tone. "I'm sure that when we hooked up last night, you knew what I was about."

"I thought I was meeting an author who had some sense. I figured the rumors were true, but this was about the book."

Marcus sucked his teeth. "It's all about the fame. You fatal-attraction book bitches are all alike, after one thing, the dick. None of you can get enough of me."

"You think I'm fatally attracted to you?" The question made her laugh. "I mean . . . sure . . . you're handsome, nicely packaged with the muscles and all, but I'm not *fatally* attracted to you." She cleared her throat as she slid into her skirt. "I'm going to go before I have your ass blacklisted." She walked by him to the stairs, her blouse half-buttoned, hose stuffed into her shirt pocket. "And it would do you some good to remember last night. You probably don't even know my name."

"Sylvia." Marcus blurted out.

"Wrong."

"Sandra?"

"Nope."

"What about Sidney?"

"Wrong again."

"Shelby?"

Silence.

Finally, she turned around. "And you call yourself the world's greatest author," she said with another laugh. "You should call yourself the world's quickest ejaculator and biggest joke with the memory of a monkey wrench. No wonder you're being boycotted."

Marcus scratched his chest. "Cut the chitchat and hurry your ass up, Sharon." Now he was grasping at straws.

"Give it up, sugar. Why don't you get my name from Regis Yeager—maybe that will ring a bell in that piece of meat you call a brain." She fluffed her hair with her hands, popped a piece of gum in her mouth, and headed down the stairs with Marcus fast at her heels.

"How do you know Regis?"

"Go to hell," she responded. She slid into a tan sweater, grabbed her briefcase, and strutted to the front door.

Now Marcus was uneasy. Unlike the average fan who just wanted a piece of him, this woman knew some of his private business. Only a person on the inside would know Regis. It made him wonder. *Who is this bitch?* Marcus made a last attempt at being polite. "Why don't you just tell me your name?"

She shot him a wry smile. "Wouldn't you like to know?" Without appearing wounded, she opened the front door, stepped on the other side, and slammed it shut without looking back.

"I don't need to know your name anyway," Marcus said to no one in particular. His apartment was silent again, and he was alone, the way he liked it. He locked the door and returned his focus to curing his hangover. The last thing he was going to worry about was some big-boned broad with a fat, dented ass who probably was just another fan like all the other desperate readers he'd slept with.

❧

Marcus went to the kitchen, where he kept his stash of medicines. He grabbed a pack of BC Headache Powder, an apple, and poured water from the tap into a small glass.

The phone rang, and Marcus met his caller with his signature greeting: "What can you do for me?"

"Hi, Marcus. This is Regis."

Happy to hear his agent's voice, Marcus grabbed an apple from the fridge and sat his naked body at the kitchen table. "Mr. Yeager, just the man I needed to talk to."

"Yeah?"

"You wouldn't believe the night I had."

"How did everything with Stephanie go?"

Marcus palmed his forehead. "Stephanie." He repeated the name. "That would have been my next guess."

"Marcus?" Regis asked, "What do you mean your *next* guess?"

"I forgot more than her name," Marcus laughed absently. "But she had an ass on her that clapped like thunder when I hit it from the back."

"Please don't tell me you had sex with Stephanie Dillon and failed to remember her name," Regis said. He sounded like he'd just found out Christmas might not be coming this year.

"Okay, I won't tell you we had sex." Marcus spoke willingly between bites. "But I will tell you we smoked, got drunk, and woke up butt-naked in my bed." Marcus laughed. "But I will not say, 'we had sex.'"

"Marcus, tell me she still wants to do business with us. Please tell me you didn't ruin another deal."

"She'll get over it."

"Get over what?"

"I had to put that bitch out of my house. She was trying to hang around. I had to make her understand that this pad is not a rest haven for hos. I have a rule that I strictly adhere to."

"Did you call her a bitch to her face?"

"I had to," Marcus said. "She woke up tripping." He bit into the apple again and talked with his mouth full. "What's her angle anyway?"

"She's one of the VIPs who has the power to green-light

movies for Beyond Films, and she wanted to option *Two Birds, One Stoned.*"

The mention of his book made Marcus sit up. He recalled dinner. "Now I remember." It was the steakhouse downtown. They both had the grilled chicken and red wine, a merlot. "Just call her back, apologize on my behalf, and ink the deal."

"Marcus, if you want me to help you accomplish any modicum of success, then you'll have to stop sabotaging your career."

Marcus didn't like what Regis had said. "You've never known me to let a piece of ass go to waste. Don't get mad at me for being me. If this Dillon chick wants to do business, then she'll call back."

"It doesn't work that way. When doing business with a woman, it's—"

"Don't give me that speech about women being different, Regis. Business is about getting in the bed with people. Who cares what happens after?"

"Some people do—that's all I'm saying."

"Whatever. These rich bitches don't care about nothing but themselves. Stephanie used sex as a bargaining tool. I just gave her what she wanted. She'll get over being called a bitch, and if she wants a blockbuster hit on her hands, she'll option *Two Birds* and you'll get your deal, Regis."

"It's not going to be that simple with Stephanie," Regis said. "I'm afraid we'll have to look elsewhere."

"Don't sound so hopeless."

"Marcus . . . you don't seem to get it. You are becoming a hard name for me to sell. Pin Oak is still talking about dropping you from your contract."

"I'm not changing the title of my next book for them—they can forget about it." Marcus bit into the apple again. "I bet they don't bother Tom Clancy or John Grisham about a fucking title."

"Marcus, your title is a bit . . . offensive."

"What's offensive about *Bitches*? The word is used a billion times every day. I think it's a great title."

"Not for selling books."

"Women writers castrate men between the pages of books every day. *Bitches* is the title of my book because my book is about some bitches," Marcus said. "I'm not changing what I wrote because a bunch of women got wind of the title, protested, and now the publishing house is afraid to take a risk."

Regis sighed. "I got the impression that the book was about a man's journey into a few bad relationships," he said.

"Right," Marcus added. "The relationships he's had with some bitches who don't give a shit about him."

"Then why not call it *Unfaithful Women*?"

"That title won't sell. Tell you what: You write your own book and call it *Unfaithful Women*. My book is done and ready."

"Your male readers can't read a book that's not out. We need to get a release date for publicity's sake."

Marcus exhaled. He was already half past frustrated. His world felt like it was closing in on him for no reason. He walked over to his floor-to-ceiling landscape window. Down below, a pack of women stood with protest signs and banners. Boycotters. They were all ages, sizes, and skin tones. Yesterday, there were less than ten; today, over twenty and counting. Marcus cradled the phone between his ear and shoulder. He tapped on the window loud enough to catch the attention of the women down below. When they looked up, he turned around and pressed his bare behind against the window long enough to get the message across. Then he stepped away and closed the blinds.

"What else you got for me?"

"Well . . ." Regis sounded apprehensive. "I was able to get you a spot on the *Lamont Troy Show,* but you have to leave this coming Friday."

"Who is Lamont Troy?"

Regis's tone became chipper and informative as he ran down what he knew. "This guy is supposedly the black Larry King of

Dallas. The show is an hour long with a live studio audience, syndicated in twenty-five markets, and carries a thirty-eight percent share of daytime viewership, which is mostly stay-at-home dads and single men. I think *Lamont Troy* is the perfect show for you."

"He sounds gay."

"He's not gay, and even if he is, I'm not asking you to sleep with him."

"Good."

"I think you should do it, but there is one little thing." Regis paused. "A boycott is being planned. If you agree, you're going to meet resistance in Dallas."

"Fuck Dallas." Marcus said. "It won't be the first time."

"Great. I'll e-mail your itinerary out tonight."

"What about *Upscale*? Am I getting the cover?"

"I called and they agreed to add you to the reading list for the fall."

"A reading list!" Marcus's jaw muscles twitched. "I want the cover!"

"The bulk of their subscribers are women, and now that *Essence* has joined the boycott against you, we have to take what we can get from the press." Regis tried to level. "Marcus, you're being ambitious right now."

"Of course I'm ambitious. This is my career we're talking about."

"It's political—you know that." Marcus could hear Regis shift papers around in the background.

"What I know is that I'm not getting any help from my goddamned agent—that's what I know."

"Dammit, Marcus, you're not exactly a contender right now. Your sales have dropped off, and the publisher doesn't feel certain releasing a book titled *Bitches* is a good move to make. Compounded with the boycott and low presale expectation, the numbers just aren't there. I need you to be more loyal to your ego and stop being so convinced that you're right about this book. Change the title or women won't buy it."

Marcus paced the floor. "My first two books sold over two hundred thousand copies to men. They bought my shit. That's where my loyalty is, to the brothers out there who are spending hard-earned dollars reading. I couldn't care less about women readers. I've managed to do what Omar Tyree, Eric Dickey, Michael Baisden, and all those other chumps couldn't. I got brothers reading popular fiction in record-breaking numbers, so don't talk to me about loyalty to my work—changing my title for a bunch of PMSing ungrateful broads is out of the question. I am convinced that I'm doing what *is* best. Now you tell those slimy sons of shit and Pin Oak to kiss my black ass. If they don't give me a release date, I'm taking them to court. Fuck the boycott, fuck women readers, and fuck you for not having faith in my work."

"Marcus, I have faith in you," Regis said. "I'm on your side."

"No, Regis, you're a leech just like everybody else who wants a piece of me and my brilliance, living off my sweat from all the hard work I put into my books. My mama didn't raise a fool, and I'm not about to start playing one."

"Your attitude betrays my efforts. How will I get you to the next level when I can't even get you to stop blocking your own way there?"

"That's for you to worry about, Shakespeare. Maybe you should stop *trying* and start *doing* for a change." Marcus was intentionally unsympathetic. "And if you can't do it, then maybe I need to find another agent."

Regis inhaled and released the breath. "Maybe you should," he said. "I mean, I'm doing my best to keep your name out there, but you have issues, Marcus . . . real issues."

"The only issue I have is being a black man in America with a nutless, big-nosed Jew for an agent."

"See what I mean?" Regis chimed in. "You're stubborn, argumentative, sexist, judgmental, neurotic, and I'm beginning to think you suffer from delusions of grandeur. Stop fucking over people, Marcus."

"I am who I am." Marcus said. "It's called keeping it real."

"Fine," Regis said in resigned frustration. "Keep it real, then."

"I knew you would see it my way, Regis."

"Actually . . . I don't." The agent's voice dropped. "I'm going to take this week to think about keeping you as a client. We'll talk when you get back."

Marcus didn't give the suggestion a second thought. "Why don't you walk the plank now, Regis? You're fired! I don't need you. Consider me a free agent as of three seconds ago. I'm not going to let some chickenshit agent or a bunch of chickenhead boycotters shatter my flow. When I get back from Dallas, I'll be making a fresh start without your assistance. Kiss my ass, Regis!"

Then, without waiting for a reply, Marcus hung up.

RAYLENE WASN'T ENJOYING CHURCH service at all. She sat between Gwena and Naomi, the three of them observing the wayward Sister Felicia Henderson make her way down the aisle.

On any given Sunday, a sermon at Mount Zephaniah Baptist always led to dramatic altar call full of shouting, praise, and good spirit-moving song, and today was no exception . . . except for one tiny detail that had Raylene chewing on her lip and pensively facing forward.

At the front of the church was Will, the head pastor—tall, sculpted, and attractive. Just looking at him gave Raylene sweaty palms, but today, she felt nothing but a knot in her gut.

It was the fifth Sunday in a row Raylene had to witness Felicia rededicate her life to Christ, which would be fine if she didn't end up in Will's embrace each and every single time.

"Thank you, Jesus!" Felicia wailed, flinging her arms with enough wild abandon to pop the top three buttons on her dress, revealing the satiny midnight blue of her bra. She wasn't even wearing a camisole.

Raylene caught Will looking.

Gwena leaned over. "If you don't do something about her, this is what his bachelor party is going to be like."

"Be quiet," Raylene whispered. She wasn't trying to hear

Gwena, who didn't even have a man. "Will would never fall for a woman like Felicia," she said. "Look at her. She's throwing herself at him. No man is going to cater to that kind of behavior. Besides, this could be Sister Henderson's turning point. She might really be coming to Christ." Raylene was sure of her words.

"If she's coming to Christ, then I'm hiding Osama bin Laden in my pocketbook," Gwena said.

Raylene didn't like the way Gwena snickered at her expense.

Naomi spoke from Raylene's left. "Come on, Ray, the Five Blind Boys of Alabama can see that she is after Pastor. Every Sunday has been like a bad rerun."

"And look at Will," Gwena added. She massaged her neck. "He's practically salivating."

Is he? Raylene stared at her fiancé. Will caught her glance, winked, and flashed a smile. *No, he isn't.* She didn't see what Naomi and Gwena thought they were seeing. What Raylene saw was a man doing his duty, bringing people closer to God. What she saw was her future with that man. Will loved *her,* and that's all that mattered, because love conquered all.

She nudged Gwena and Naomi away. "No matter what you two think you *might* be seeing, this is an act of the holy spirit, and it should be taken seriously."

Gwena and Naomi backed off.

However, Raylene still felt the knot as Felicia passed the second pew from the front. It was where the three sat, and something seemed horrendously intentional about what was repeatedly going on before her eyes.

From the musician's pit, Raylene was met with two more hard stares, one from Sister Latice Harris, who was playing the organ, and the other from Sister Thelma Wade, who was in the choir stand, singing. It was Thelma's voice that usually brought the house down, and today was no exception as she bellowed a soulful original and church favorite.

This mess I'm in
ain't nothing but sin
and the only way out
is to not give in
and when I'm through
I'll say amen
because this battle
will be over
by and by.

Felicia danced and shouted, spoke in tongues, and shook her rump and hips like a runway model at a jig fest. Her energy seemed contagious, and before long, four other members of the congregation were up shouting as well.

"Jesuuuuuuuus!" Felicia's biting scream sailed through the church, along with the sound of drums, tambourine, organ, and guitar. The place began to rock, but the three women in the second pew weren't impressed, and neither were Sisters Harris and Wade.

"That's a shame," Gwena said. "Sister Henderson's bra doesn't even match her dress. If this were the chocolate factory, she'd be Willy Wonka."

Raylene was the only one who found Gwena's sense of humor humorless.

Naomi convulsed with silent laughter. "And who still wears gold-plated name necklaces?"

"Somebody needs to call the fashion police."

Raylene scolded. "Will you two stop?"

When Felicia had danced and shouted her way to the front, where Will stood, she fell at the pastor's feet. He carefully pulled her up from the floor and cradled her in his arms. Then, and only then, did Raylene see it. Will wasn't just holding on to Felicia, he'd taken a few seconds to embrace her, letting her whisper something into his ear and smiling in agreement. Will didn't just grin from behind his lips this time, he was showing teeth. He pat-

ted Sister Henderson's hand and released her to the ushers standing nearby. Raylene tried to catch his eye again, but this time,
Will stepped into the pulpit and drank his water. The entire scene
made Raylene shift uncomfortably in the pew like a child in a
tight to go to the bathroom.

"You need to do something about him, Ray," Naomi said. "If
that were Vincent, I'd check him so fast, he'd think he was the
only option box on a multiple-choice test."

"One thing's for sure: It's obvious what Felicia wants, and it's
obvious she doesn't care about him being engaged," Gwena said.

Raylene shot the two with a warning stare. "I'm not going to
ask you two again to please stop. Don't you think if something
were up with Will that I would know? His heart is with me at all
times. He's a man of God, not some boyfriend from high
school."

"Fe Henderson isn't after his heart, Ray. She knows you have
that. Heck, the whole world knows you have Will Robinson's
heart," Naomi added. "What Felicia is after has nothing to do
with Will being a man of God. I know. I see this kind of thing
play out on *Judge Mathis* all the time."

"*Judge Mathis?*" Raylene huffed. "Girl, please."

"I'm serious. Women like Fe don't care about God. All they
care about is getting a piece of whatever man they have the hots
for at the moment. I've had to run enough hoochie mamas away
from my honey to know."

Naomi's husband was a guitar player with enough good looks
to get any woman heated between the legs. Naomi had told them
stories of having to fight women to keep her husband.

Gwena nudged Raylene. "See, even Naomi knows better."

Raylene nodded in annoyed disagreement. Naomi was young
and still had a lot to learn about being in a healthy relationship.
Fighting had never been a resolve in Raylene's book for keeping a
man, and she wasn't about to consider it now. "I'm thirty-four,
not twenty. I'm not going to fight a woman for Will. He knows
we're getting married; therefore, he knows better."

Naomi exhaled. "Age means nothing. Sometimes you will have to fight for your man, especially if you have a good one."

Gwena leaned over Raylene and whispered to Naomi. She was so close, Raylene could smell the White Diamonds perfume she wore. "Maybe if you stopped watching so much television, you wouldn't have to fight women off your husband."

"At least I have a husband, Gwena," Naomi shot back. "When are you going to get one?"

"You didn't have to go there."

"And you didn't have to go where you went."

"All I was saying was if you would pay more attention to Vincent that your life would be all right."

"My life *is* all right."

Raylene looked at Naomi. "Gwena does have a point."

"Don't you start in on me, Miss Goody Two-shoes," Naomi said. "I'm not the one sitting in church watching my fiancé get raped by a woman with the Holy Ghost."

The music came to a low crescendo, and Will raised his arms to calm the congregation. The gesture seemed appropriate for the bantering going on in the second pew.

"Let the church say amen," he said.

Raylene straightened to attention. One day soon, she would be the first lady over everything she was a part of right now. She'd be responsible each Sunday for making sure Will was ready to lead his flock, even if it meant putting her interiors business on the back burner, which she was prepared to do. Being a preacher's wife was something she'd always imagined herself to be, and Raylene could already see that it was going to require a certain amount of strength and gumption that she was sure she had. She didn't consider herself the dramatic type, but maybe she was going to start having to be more like Naomi and let women know where the line was drawn.

Will spoke into the microphone. "The Lord has been good," he said, smiling. "We have fifteen lambs of God coming before us today to join or rejoin with Jesus."

Applause erupted throughout the sanctuary. Getting new members was always good news. Mount Zephaniah was growing.

Sister Henderson released herself from the grip of the ushers and moved back over to Will. Like a child, she latched on to his arm, clutching it as if it were the last life jacket on a boat full of people. Felicia then shot Raylene a cursory glance before sliding her hand into his.

Will shifted awkwardly away from Sister Henderson before introducing her. "First, coming to testify, we have Sister Felicia Henderson, who is a member of our church and who has been in the fire like Daniel in the lion's den these past few months on her job, and she's come to rededicate herself to the Lord."

Felicia all but snatched the microphone from his hand.

From the choirstand, Latice looked at Raylene as she lowered the music so they could all hear what was about to come out of Sister Henderson's mouth. Her look was suspicious and condemning enough to make Raylene drop her eyes. Felicia Henderson spoke between sniffs into the mic.

"First, I give honor to the Lord and Savior Jesus Christ for without whom I would not be here." She cracked a few tearful breaths and then snuggled into the cup of the pastor's supportive shoulder. "I just want to thank God for our pastor, Reverend Robinson. He's a kind man and a true man of God who I just felt like getting up and celebrating today. He's been counseling me, and it's been only through him and Jesus that I've gotten down on my knees and became humbled enough to let the Lord back into my life. You see, I was a sinner. . . ."

Raylene felt Naomi back in her ear. "She's disrespecting you, Ray. Today after church you need to talk to Will."

"This is Will's job." Raylene put her defenses up. "I will not bring insinuation and bad energy to his job."

The last thing Raylene wanted to do was confront Will about a gut feeling. That's how she lost her last boyfriend, who called her paranoid, insecure, and psychotic. Of course, that was after she had him followed, only to discover that Todd really was away in New Orleans on business. She wasn't willing to risk the same thing with Will. What if she was wrong and ended up losing another perfectly good man to her own insecurity? She was tired of being alone, and at some point she had to trust she was with a man who told her the truth. She believed in Will's words and had no reason not to, other than that of a gut feeling. It was probably just gas.

"Then take it to the house," Naomi said. "Talk to him when you get home tonight."

"I think you need to have a talk with Felicia," Gwena added. "She's the one who needs to be checked. That would rectify all of this."

Raylene got up and excused herself. She didn't want to appear bothered, but the stress of sitting there was on her like heartburn. Gwena and Naomi followed her out. She wasn't even at the water fountain before they were pestering her again.

"Raylene, why are you running?"

"I'm not running, Nay." Raylene attempted a front. "I just needed some water."

"You and Will need to talk," Gwena said. Now that they could speak without whispering, the raspy high alto of her voice was clear. "You need to put a stop to this before you get married. It's apparent this makes you uncomfortable. What are you going to do when this congregation grows to fifteen thousand instead of five hundred and women are coming out of the woodwork?"

"Will won't let it get out of hand," Raylene heard herself say. "I trust him. Besides, what would I be putting a stop to? Felicia Henderson has a right to seek guidance from the pastor of the church."

"Great. Now you wanna act like a Stepford Wife before you even have the ring," Naomi said. She touched Raylene on the shoulder. "It's already out of hand. You need to let your man know that this is bothering you and stop being so passive and unassuming."

"Either that or check that Jezebel." Gwena's face was adamant. It was no secret that she disliked Felicia Henderson.

Raylene rolled her eyes and went off. She was tired of defending herself and Will. "Will you two stop it? Will is a grown man, and I'm not worried about Sister Henderson, okay? Thank you very much. Now, get out of my business, please."

"Excuse us, Superwoman," Gwena said. "Consider the conversation officially closed."

Raylene checked her watch. There was no use in going back inside; church would be ending in a matter of minutes. She caught Gwena massaging her neck again. Her friend looked preoccupied and unable to knock whatever was on her mind.

"What's bothering you?"

"Friday."

Raylene remembered. "The Marcus Brooks interview?"

"Yes. I'm actually nervous, and I'm only a camera op." Gwena rolled her neck in an effort to remove the tension. "People are already calling the station harassing us. We're being boycotted."

Raylene shook her head. "I don't know why you don't just call in sick. You know every book club in Dallas is boycotting, us included."

"I have a job to do," Gwena said. "And Marcus Brooks isn't going to keep me from doing my job." Her words were stiff and deliberate. Her hurt was invisible. "I'll be okay."

"Maybe you should visit the spa this week," Raylene suggested. "It might do your neck and hands some good."

"I probably will." Gwena continued the massage as she spoke to Naomi.

"Are you boycotting?"

"I can't. Friday mornings are my busiest days at the salon," Naomi said. "But I have a surprise for the book club." She reached into her purse and took out an envelope. "I know we're supposed to be discussing Pearl Cleage on Friday night, but I have tickets to go see Common Folk, D'Angelo, and the Jazzyfatnastees at the Gypsy Tea Room Friday."

Gwena's eyebrows shot up in surprise. "That is good news."

"Common Folk is my favorite band!" Raylene gawked in disbelief. The lineup excited her. "Did you get an extra ticket for Will?" she asked.

"No," Naomi said defensively. "I didn't. This is girls' night out. Members of Second Pew only. Why would you want to ruin our night with old corny Will?"

"Yeah, why would you want to ruin our night?" Gwena asked. If she had not been grinning, Raylene would have taken offense.

Raylene raised an eyebrow. "Will is not corny."

Naomi rolled her eyes. "Yes, he is. Any man that has to have a bowl of Malt-O-Meal before he goes to bed every night is corny."

Raylene regretted ever telling Naomi about Will's odd habits. Whenever the hairstylist got the chance, she reminded Raylene how she felt about Will.

"Will is corny," Gwena agreed. "But who gives a shit?"

Raylene let out a startled gasp. "We're still in church, you know."

"I'm sorry," Gwena said as she huffed. "My mind is on other things."

"Like Marcus Brooks?"

"Among other things."

Raylene sympathized. "I know what you mean. Sometimes I wish Felicia Henderson was at another church."

Naomi held up her hands. "Hey, we're supposed to be celebrating going out on Friday, not talking about those two." She looked at Gwena. "And you need to stop swearing in church. It's not cute."

"I apologized once already," Gwena said. "What do you want me to do? Three hundred Hail Marys?"

Raylene looked at the floor. Her face dropped its cheerfulness. "I don't think that works in a missionary Baptist church." Naomi laughed. "But you could stand to have your mouth washed out with soap."

"Maybe I shouldn't go to the concert," Raylene said. Her face had lost the excitement it held just seconds before. "Will doesn't like me listening to anything that isn't gospel, and I try to honor that."

"What would Will know?" Naomi said in a casual tone. "He was probably conceived to the gospel according to Marvin Gaye."

The women laughed.

"Have you told Latice and Thelma?" Raylene asked.

"Not yet."

Gwena tossed her thick curls behind her ears. "We'll have to drag Latice out of the house."

"All I need to say is *D'Angelo,* and Latice forgets she's a forty-three-year-old single mother." Naomi smiled. "We won't have to do much coaxing."

"It will also give her a reason to give Lance some space. She smothers and spoils him so."

Raylene retrieved her compact from her purse to touch up her makeup while she talked. "Gwena, her only son is about to go off to school. She'll be all alone. Of course she's a little clingy right now."

"That's all the more reason to spend time preparing to be alone rather than fighting the inevitability of it." Gwena argued. "The boy is going to college in the fall, and the quicker Latice accepts it, the better."

Raylene disliked Gwena's unsympathetic attitude sometimes. "Don't you have any shame about you?"

"Let me check," Gwena said. She stood still several seconds before looking back at Raylene. "I guess I don't."

"Okay," Naomi interrupted. "Let me go home so I can see about my boys and cook them dinner. Vincent acts like he's allergic to cleaning up when he's not on the road."

"Tell him we said hi and thanks for the tickets," Gwena said.

They watched Naomi exit the building.

"She is so lucky," Raylene said. "Vincent is fine, he loves her dirty drawers, he's given her two beautiful sons, and he plays backup guitar for some of the best musicians around."

Gwena shifted her weight to one leg. "Yeah, but Naomi takes him for granted. It's a miracle he's been around this long. She treats him like he's one of the kids."

"You really need to stop," Raylene said. "Don't you ever say anything without that biting sarcasm of yours?"

Gwena stood back on one leg. "Admit it, Ray. That night the book club went to the movies and Naomi brought Vincent against his will only to nail him to the cross in front of us for not paying attention. It was embarrassing for all of us. Not to mention, she's always telling their business. At the last book club meeting, I didn't care to know that Vincent walked around the house in nothing but briefs full of holes."

"So," Raylene said. "She's married, and that's what married women do. *We* talk about *our* husbands."

"You're not married." Raylene felt Gwena's eyes on her. She looked like she was withholding information. She didn't know what Gwena was getting at, but it didn't feel like a compliment.

"Three weeks and counting," Raylene said. "The wedding is right around the corner, so I might as well be. The ceremony is a technicality."

"There's always room for error."

"Not when you take your time and do it right. I'm not Naomi."

"You sure have it all figured out," Gwena said.

"I wouldn't say that, but we both know Naomi's wedding was drama. Vincent was late, and when he did show up, he had to tell Naomi about Tiffany. How would you like to find out on your wedding day that your husband has fathered a child with another woman? Not to mention that the twins and Sierra were born the same month of the same year. I'm not making that mistake."

"Naomi didn't make a mistake either."

"You know what I mean." Raylene hated feeling like she had to defend herself, but Gwena had a tendency to act like she didn't get it.

"First of all, I'm not walking down the aisle with five months' worth of baby in my belly, and I'm not nineteen. Naomi was young when she got married. She hadn't even voted in her first presidential election. She and Vincent never had time to themselves. She walked over the threshold and into the maternity ward. For all we know, Vincent married her because of the pregnancy."

"So, she's managed to make her marriage last for six years, and he's still with her. That should account for something."

"Tell that to Whitney Houston and Bobby Brown. I'm not impressed."

"Maybe you should be," Gwena snapped. "Maybe you should observe how Naomi manages to make her union with Vince work."

"Situations like Nay's *never* last."

Gwena asked. "How do you know so much without the experience? I think you have gotten beside yourself with this by-the-book thinking. Men don't like living by the book, and the sooner you realize that, the better off you will be."

"What?" Raylene had become lost in her own thoughts. Sometimes Gwena got on her nerves, and she had to tune her out.

The double doors leading to the sanctuary opened, and a flood of people began to exit.

"Never mind." Gwena walked over, kissed and hugged Raylene. "I'll see you Friday, girl. Have a good week."

She watched Gwena exit.

Raylene found herself lost in a sea of faces—some she knew, some she didn't. She headed for the pastor's study to wait for Will. It was the normal routine. She'd go, sit, and read her notes from the day's sermon until he showed up.

"Hey, Sister Nix."

Raylene turned and saw Latice. The women hugged. Raylene was happy to see her because it meant having someone to talk to. It meant the time waiting for Will wouldn't be so long or lonely.

"The choir wore it out today," she said. "All praise to Thelma," Latice added with a grin. "She's the one. Every Sunday, it's her singing that keeps our membership up. I almost couldn't play the song for the foolishness that was going on down front and center. When are you going to say something?"

"Not you too," Raylene's voice begged. "Naomi and Gwena have given me an earful already."

"Because we can't stand the eyeful." Latice nodded toward the stairs leading to the bottom of the church. "I'm on my way to the basement to get an extra choir robe from storage. Care to walk with me?"

"Sure." Raylene couldn't think of anything better.

The corridors were long with many doors. Some were classroom doors, others storage and offices.

Latice jingled the keys that were in her hand. As lead musician for the church, she owned a set of keys to every door in the building. It was something Raylene knew she'd get once she and Will married.

"Was it Felicia Henderson who wanted to join the choir?" Raylene asked as they walked. She tried to sound as if she didn't care, but she did. It was important for her to know Sister Henderson's moves just in case she really was after Will.

Latice cringed. "I wouldn't let Felicia Henderson in my choir if Jesus himself commissioned me to," she said.

Raylene laughed. It felt good to laugh. "Where is Thelma? I wanted to tell her that she jammed that song this morning."

"She had to rush home. Girl, people are coming into her neighborhood stealing expensive dogs and reselling them bootleg on the street. She left to check on Monroe."

Raylene shook her head. "That's a shame."

"I don't know why people gotta steal from other people. It's like the Atlanta child murders of the Dallas dog world," Latice said. "Thelma is consumed with helping the police catch the culprits. She heads up the neighborhood watch and went so far as to design and make customized collars for each of the dogs on her street."

"Good for her. Maybe she can make Felicia a collar."

Latice looked at Raylene begrudgingly. "Speaking of which, I hope you're planning to talk to Will about Sister Henderson's behavior."

"Guess what? We're all going to see D'Angelo at the Gypsy Tea Room on Friday," Raylene said in an attempt to avoid the subject.

Latice's mouth dropped open. Excitement showed and then disappeared from her face. She pointed at Raylene. "Don't think I've let you off the hook. Did you say D'Angelo, as in my favorite male singer?"

"Yes, ma'am. Vincent gave Naomi five tickets." Raylene liked being the bearer of good news.

"I'll leave my house for D'Angelo," Latice said. "I can't believe we have tickets. What am I going to wear?"

The women walked down a second flight, then a third. "Now I remember why I never come down here," Raylene said as she looked around. "It's creepy."

"It's not so creepy a place when you find out it's where the teens hang out. Two years ago, I caught Lance and Christy down here rubbing up against each other, carrying on like dogs in heat. He just got off punishment yesterday."

Raylene laughed. "I never knew that," she said. "They make such a cute couple. I think it's adorable when young people are in love."

"Wait until you have kids. Then you'll see it ain't all so cute or adorable. I am not prepared to be a grandmother, and I work hard at making sure my son doesn't make me one."

The stairs seemed never-ending.

Latice slowed down. "I really don't mind being a big girl until I get near some steps or any kind of incline—then I regret it," she said.

Raylene could hear Latice's breathing. It filled the air between the clicking echoes of their heels against the floor.

"Then do something about it. It's nothing a little cardio won't fix."

"That's easy for you to say, Ray. You're fit as a fiddle, toned, and curved in all the right places. I could stand to run a few laps."

Running was Raylene's favorite thing to do when she found an ounce of time to herself. Running not only kept her thin, but it also kept her sane, being outside letting her feet take her from one destination to another. However, since she'd moved in with Will and started her own interior design business, she rarely if ever made time anymore. *Where did the time go?* Still, Raylene remained optimistic for Latice. "Just pray about it, Tice. God knows what's on your heart about your weight."

"I need to do more than pray." Latice said. "I bought a two-year membership to the twenty-four-hour gym up the street from my house. I just need to motivate myself to go."

"No better time than the present."

Latice revealed a dimpled grin. "I think about it while eating Oreos in bed watching *Oprah* on TiVo."

Raylene cracked up. Latice was funny, smart, wise, and a joy to be around.

"Will you be able to make the boycott?"

"I don't think so." Raylene wrinkled her nose at Latice. "Marcus Brooks isn't worthy for consideration onto my calendar, I'm sorry, but I have a wedding to plan, and I just don't see this whole boycott issue as important."

Latice stopped. "Maybe if you had a son to raise, you wouldn't be saying that."

"Maybe," Raylene said. "But I don't."

Latice's laugh was cynical.

"Thelma would agree with me. She doesn't really want to do the boycott either."

"Really?"

"She's only going because none of us can and you made such a big deal about it at the last book club meeting. She'd rather be at work. As a matter of fact, she's going in early Friday morning before the boycott, and she's not even on the schedule. And Gwena, of course, is only doing her job by going in. I guess we're just a bunch of women who prefer work over standing out in the hot sun to protest a man that isn't worth the time of day to be angry about."

Latice frowned. "You all can be so half-assed sometimes. At the last meeting, everyone was fired up, and now today I'm hearing excuses."

Raylene took in a deep breath and released it. She had to keep it real. "I'm just telling you the truth," she said. "You're the only one who really wants to be there but can't. Not unless you're faking it too."

"No, I'm not faking it," Latice said. "I really think this is something to make the sacrifice for if you can. It's important that Marcus knows his former fans are not going to tolerate his arrogance. If it weren't for book clubs and women who read, he'd never be the success he is. Since my part-time job laid me off, I've got to work overtime at the PD to make sure Lance never has to worry about them pulling the rug from under him in college."

"But you know Thelma's got your back, Tice." Raylene smiled. "She'll be there if she says she's going to be there, and you want to know how I know?"

"How?"

"Because I'm going to make plans to be there with her."

"Thank you!" Latice embraced Raylene and rocked her cheerfully.

Raylene playfully pushed away as they reached the door to the choir closet. "Okay, okay, that's enough Miss Mushy. Let's go get this choir robe."

The door was ajar.

"I brought these keys for nothing," Latice said.

Raylene stepped into the darkness and felt against the wall for the light. The room smelled damp and salty. She made a mental note to tell Will to get some of the trustees of the church to come down and do some cleaning. The women heard shuffling.

Raylene felt Latice's hands grab her arm. The grip was so tight, it startled her. "We're not alone in here."

"Then let me turn on the light before I get scared," Raylene said. She reached over and pulled the string inside the closet.

There between the robes was Felicia Henderson on her knees with Will's penis protruding from her mouth like an oversize stick of peppermint. Her eyes bucked with surprise.

"Well, I'll be damned," Latice said in a stunned voice.

Will stumbled backward against the rack where several robes now lay on the floor in a neat pile where he and Felicia had been lying. His pants and boxer briefs were at his ankles and his eyes were wide with alarm. He tried to talk, but only stumbled through an explanation attempt. "Raylene . . . Sister Harris . . . I was just . . . uh . . . praying with Sister Henderson here."

Felicia stood up and wiped the shine from her mouth. Her blue bra was now loose and hanging from her arms, her dress around her waist. She blinked like a deer in headlights, but there was no remorse on her face. Her eyes remained cold and empty.

Shock ran so heavy through Raylene, she had to lean against the wall. Her feet felt as if they had melted into the floor. In this instant, she wanted to be gone, to disappear. Raylene wished she'd never accepted Latice's invitation to walk to the basement.

Felicia latched her bra closed and pulled her dress back onto her shoulders. She was bony and top heavy, nothing like Raylene. *What does Will see in her?*

Will quickly pulled up his pants. The sound of the zipper

seemed amplified in Raylene's ears. He stepped over to her, his arms outstretched. "This is not what it looks like."

Raylene stepped away, still silent and unable to speak.

"Oh, really?" Latice said. "It looks like two people getting it on in the church choir closet. Am I wrong?"

Felicia grabbed her purse and zipped past Raylene, bumping her slightly but with bold intention.

Raylene smelled the cologne Will wore in the breeze that Sister Henderson had left behind. It was Grey Flannel, the scent Raylene loved to smell against his skin.

Latice stopped Felicia from passing by her. "You ought to be ashamed of yourself," she said in a fussing tone before finally letting her go.

Felicia walked out with her head down.

Will buttoned his shirt. "Raylene, I'm . . . sorry."

"Yeah, you're sorry all right," Raylene heard herself say as she charged him and whacked him across the face, sending him flailing a second time into the rack. She felt her eyes sting with the heat of tears as she ran from the basement. She was embarrassed and felt small. Outside, the sun made her feel like she was center stage for all the world to see and laugh at. She climbed into her car, sat, and cried until she heard a knock on the glass. It was Latice. Raylene rolled down the window.

She leaned against the car panting. She smiled. "I'm not designed for chasing you down." Latice reached into her dress pocket and retrieved some tissue. "Here."

Raylene smiled wearily as she wiped the tears and snot from her face. Her eyes felt tired and swollen.

"Are you going to be okay?"

Raylene shook her head.

Latice reached in and gave Raylene a comforting touch on the shoulder. "Call me if you need me, and you know you can always camp out on the couch at my place. It's not much, but Lance and I would love to have you."

"I can handle it." Raylene shook her head and feigned an I'm-trying-to-cope grin. "I'll be okay." She put the key in the ignition, started up the car, and drove away.

After one night in the house with Will, Raylene moved out. She couldn't handle it. All the prayer in the last twenty-four hours wasn't enough to make her forgive, though she tried. By Friday, she was no closer to forgiving or forgetting. All Raylene knew was that she hurt and she didn't ever want to hurt like that again.

THELMA FINISHED HER MORNING ROUNDS at the animal hospital before leaving to go to the television station. She'd been waiting for this day all week. Things at the hospital had been quiet all morning, and she was glad to see a German shepherd and an iguana released from ICU under her care. As she did everything else, Thelma took her veterinary job seriously.

"Okay, everyone, I'm leaving." Thelma removed her doctor's coat and hung it on a coat rack near the nurses' station.

The staff gathered around their head physician and began cheering her on. "Go get 'em, girl!" one nurse said as she approached. "Shut Marcus Brooks down!"

A doctor with skin the color of desert sand grabbed Thelma's hand in her own and squeezed it firmly as she said, "And, Dr. Wade, make sure you mention that the all-female staff of Peoples' Victory Animal Hospital over here in uptown Dallas are protesting in spirit."

Everyone cheered.

"I hope they get you on television saying it," another staff member said. She waved her arm banded with sterling-silver bracelets in the air. "And you tell Marcus Brooks that he doesn't just get to put out his preachy, same-old trifling-ass black man stories and expect us to pay for it with our hard-earned consumer dollars!"

The room broke into a crash of cheers. Women were beating

on the desk, stomping their feet, whistling, and cheering a send-off victory as Thelma led the uproar.

They hardly noticed the frail, coconut-shell-colored woman who had come running in with blood trickling down her neck. She was shabbily dressed, smelled like hot garbage, and her hair was in cornrows. She wasn't from the uptown area, from the looks of her thrift-store clothes and unkempt appearance.

"Excuse me," she said, breaking up the celebratory send-off. "I got a dog bite, and I needs it looked at." The woman's eyes caught Thelma's. "Do you have an eyeball problem?"

Ashamed that she'd been caught staring, Thelma apologized. "My bad," she said.

"Yeah, yo' bad," the woman snapped back. "Now, are any of you going to help me, or do I have to be foaming at the mouth and have fur down my back to get some attention?"

Thelma stepped up. "Ma'am, this is an animal hospital."

The woman whipped around and looked at her. "Did I ask you what kind of hospital this was? I can see that it's a place for animals. I got bit by one—don't you think I know that?"

One of the nurses ran up to assist the woman, walking her away from the entrance and over to the waiting area. The woman scoped the place out as she was being escorted to a chair. "Man, this some nice fancy hospital. Parkland don't look nothing like this. Is that real water coming out of that fountain?"

Thelma smiled at the comment. "Yes, it is."

Then the woman frowned. "Don't y'all believe in having men around?" she asked. Then she gestured as if she understood. "Oh, I see this is an animal hospital run by lesbians." She nodded. "I'm cool with it. But I don't get down like that. Just look at my injury, and I'll be on my straight way."

"This is not a staff of lesbians. We just happen to be an all-female staff," Thelma said as she walked over, regarding the woman curiously. "What do you do?"

"I'm a con . . . conservationist."

Thelma shot her a look of disbelief. The woman didn't even

look like she could spell *conservationist,* let alone be one. Suspicion made a home in Thelma's stomach. She wanted to know what a transient-looking woman was doing in such an exclusive neighborhood with a dog bite to the neck.

She checked her watch. There was enough time to look at the wound herself. She took over, excused the nurse, and escorted the woman into a small examination room.

"I'm Thelma Wade, the head doctor."

"How do you do, Thelma Wade," the woman responded. Her voice was more of a cackle than coherent speech with standard English. "I don't know many folk named Thelma, and those that I do know, they ain't young at all."

"Can I see the bite?" Thelma asked.

The woman leaned over and revealed a gash on her neck near her collarbone. "Looks like I had it out with a baby vampire, don't it?"

Thelma checked the wound. It looked worse than it was. The marks were clean, small, and as far as she could tell, nothing that a good alcohol cleaning and a Band-Aid couldn't fix, provided the dog wasn't rabid. "What kind of dog was it?"

"Well, I can't rightly say." The woman's accent went flat. "But he was small enough for me to hold him on my shoulder like a baby, you know?"

"Was he a puppy?"

"I don't know." The woman gritted her teeth and clamped her eyes shut when the alcohol swab contacted the wound.

Thelma was careful as she worked. "It's hard to believe you have a dog and don't know what breed it is."

"The dog . . . was a gift," she sputtered. "I named him Woody."

"That's a nice name," Thelma said. "Speaking of names, what is yours?"

"Oh, no," the woman said. "I don't give out my name to nobody. I only give my name out for shit like emergencies. You know, like winning the lottery or the Publishers Clearing House."

"What about life-and-death matters? Wouldn't you give your name for that?"

"As long as I'm alive and know my own name, that's all that matters. And when I'm dead, it ain't gonna matter at all." The woman flashed a grin of superiority.

"Did you aggravate the dog?"

"Well, not really. Woody was new and probably just not used to me yet. I'm the kind of person who don't really care for pets, but he was a gift. I guess he didn't want me picking his little ass up. Imagine that. I don't even have chemistry with a dog. No wonder I don't have a man." The woman laughed at her joke.

"You said was . . . is the dog still alive?"

"Oh yeah, that booger is still alive, well, and in his own back-yard."

Thelma's curiosity only grew. "Where'd you get him?"

"I just told you he was a gift. I even got this cute orange collar so he can be pimped out like me. You know orange is my favorite color."

"Orange must be in this year," Thelma said as she cleaned the wound.

"It must be," the woman said. "The collar that my dog wears is this cute little orange customized number with gold coins spray-painted on it with a touch of those shells that they wear over in Africa."

"They are called cowry shells, and they're sixteenth-century French coins." Thelma knew the collar. She'd made it herself. The woman had stolen the dog. Describing the collar in such detail had given it away.

The dog was a mouse schnauzer, the latest crossbred fad in purse pets, running owners upward of two thousand dollars a pop. Buster was the dog's real name, and he belonged to a neighbor of Thelma's who lived four houses down.

When the woman saw that Thelma couldn't be fooled any longer, she attempted to flee, but she was no match for Thelma's powerful grip. "Please don't turn me in!" the woman begged. "I'll tell you my name."

"Tell it to the police. I'm turning you in."

"Sister, I'm already on probation." The woman begged, "You ain't gonna send an old woman to jail, is you?"

Thelma had no sympathy for the woman, who looked no older than fifty-five or so. "Where's the dog?"

"The hell I know," she said. "He bit me, and I dropped him back in the yard where I got him from. That's the God's to honest truth."

Thelma picked up the phone to call the police. Then one of the nurses rushed into the room. "Dr. Wade, the shepherd amputee is going into cardiac arrest. We need you right away!" The nurse rushed back down the hall.

Instinctively, Thelma moved to see to the emergency but paused when she realized she couldn't trust her dog thief to sit and wait for her to return.

"Watcha gonna do, huh?" The woman tried to persuade Thelma. "Is you going to let the dog die or let me go? My suggestion is you let me go, huh? C'mon, Wade, how about it?"

Thelma was a doctor first, and the life of any animal put in her hands wasn't put on hold for anything. "Tell me your name, and I'll release you."

"You promise?"

"Scout's honor."

"Jonnie . . . Jonnie Coleman."

"If another dog comes up missing in my neighborhood, Jonnie Coleman, I'm going to find you, and I'm going to grab you by that scrawny little neck of yours and walk you in the cops myself. Understood?"

"You ain't gotta worry about me," Jonnie said. "I promise. My dog-snatching days is over, and I don't break a promise." She scratched her head curiously. "What about my bite?"

"You'll be fine. Just keep it clean and get some ointment to put on it." Thelma grabbed the stethoscope from her desk and sprinted down the hall toward the emergency room.

Six hours later, Thelma emerged from the doors of the hospital tired and ready to go home. It had been a longer day than expected. The German shepherd could not be saved, she'd lost the dog-thieving woman, and worst of all, she'd missed the boycott.

When Thelma pulled up to her house, Raylene's car was in the driveway. The BMW gave her house a prosperous look. Especially against her own pearl-colored SUV. She wondered if Raylene was up yet. Last night, Thelma had to give her uptight friend a Valium so she could sleep instead of crying in hysterics every time she saw or heard something that reminded her of Will.

"Hey, hey! I'm home," Thelma said as she entered the house. Then she began to whistle.

A black Labrador came trotting from the back of the house. He jumped up on Thelma and began licking her face.

Thelma ruffled his fur. "Hey, Monroe," she said. "How's my boy today?"

The dog let himself down and sat diligently waiting for Thelma. She walked toward her room.

Raylene appeared from the hallway. She was all cleaned up, but Thelma could tell from the dull look in Raylene's eyes that she needed the outing more than she wanted it. Thelma hugged her best friend. "How are you feeling?"

"Fine now that I'm all cried out with no place to go," she joked. "That pill you gave me had me going toward the light or something, because I didn't wake up until four fifteen this afternoon. I slept through the demonstration."

Thelma smiled. "You needed the rest and so did I. Since you've left Will and haven't told anyone that you're over here, you've really been getting on my nerves."

"Thelma Wade, how can you say that about me?"

"Easily. You haven't left this house all week, and when you're not crying like a three-year-old over Will, you're talking about him." Thelma walked over and hugged Raylene gently. "There's only so much I can take," she said. "I had to give you something."

Thelma released Raylene and checked her out. "Is that a new outfit?"

Raylene looked down at herself. "Sort of. I got it for my birthday last year. Will picked it out. Do you like it?"

Thelma looked down at Monroe. "What do you think?"

Monroe growled and licked his paws.

"He says that I need to send your ass back home to Will." Thelma smiled. Raylene didn't find the joke amusing. Thelma leaned down and gave Monroe some extra petting. "You're such a good man. Yes, you are."

"Don't you mean *pet?* He's such a good pet?"

Thelma shook her head and walked into her room. "No, I mean he's a good man like I said. Monroe is a full-grown male dog. He's a man."

Raylene followed. She came in and sat on the bed next to Thelma. "So does that make you a bitch instead of a woman?"

Thelma cut her eyes at Raylene. "Maybe. Look, I had a hard day. I didn't make the boycott either." Thelma's voice was full of disappointment. "Right before I was leaving, some cranky woman who I believe was the neighborhood dog thief came in with a dog bite, and then one of my patients went into cardiac arrest. It was emergency surgery and funeral plans from there." She kicked off her shoes. "I hope Latice won't be too mad that Second Pew's representatives weren't there to represent."

Raylene picked lint from her top. "She'll understand."

"Did you call Will today?" Thelma asked.

"No."

"Why not?"

"I need time." Raylene's voice shook. "I wouldn't know where to begin if I called him."

"How about, 'Why the fuck did you cheat on me?' for starters?"

"I can't just say that."

"Well . . . you have a wedding to either get through or cancel, and you can't stay with me forever rent-free, crying and keeping me up at night," Thelma said.

"I know."

Thelma caught the sadness in Raylene's tone, so she ceased the joking around. Thelma questioned the bloodred velvet-covered notebook hiked under Raylene's arm. "What is that?"

"It's my journal."

Thelma gave Raylene a doubtful look. "When did you start keeping a journal?" She laughed. "I thought only two kinds of people kept journals: one-eyed sea captains and Oprah-cultists."

"Then call me a cultist," Raylene said. "But I love it. You need to keep a journal." She offered Thelma more words of advice: "It might help you release some of that aggression you have inside from not having a real man."

"Excuse me?"

"Well," Raylene stammered. "It's obvious that you're substituting a relationship with a dog for a real one with a man."

"That's where you're wrong," Thelma snapped. "I'm happy being single. Monroe is in my life because I love animals. I wouldn't be a vet if I didn't." Then she smiled. "Besides, it's a fact that single people with pets live longer and stay much happier."

"But that's not true love or companionship," Raylene commented.

"It certainly isn't having your preacher fiancé being caught in a closet getting a blow job by another woman either," Thelma replied.

When Thelma saw that Raylene wasn't as tough as she figured her to be, a rush of guilt went through her. She softened up. "Raylene, I'm sorry. I didn't mean to go there."

Raylene wiped tears from her eyes. "Girl, don't worry. It's the truth, and that's why this is so hard on me—because I really do love Will."

"I know you do," Thelma said. "But he's made it obvious that he's not in love with you."

Raylene stared at nothing in particular. "Maybe it was my fault."

"Don't start blaming yourself."

"But . . . maybe Gwena was right. Maybe I should have gotten ghetto and . . . I don't know . . . talked to Felicia."

"Maybe it is better that you didn't. God helped you out by having you walk into that basement Sunday morning."

"I suppose, but why do I feel so dismantled?"

Thelma nudged her friend. "Because you're human and you've been emotionally crushed. Now do you see why I prefer living with a dog? Men are too much of a fucking pain in the neck." She patted Raylene's shoulder, got up, and prepared to take a shower. "If it's a man you want, Raylene, you have to go out and *choose him*. Don't let him choose you. That way, you know what you're getting."

"But that's not the way it's supposed to happen. The man is supposed to woo the woman. I refuse to act desperate."

"Stop living in la-la land." Then, as if she'd forgotten to say something. "You don't *need* him—you know that, right?"

"What are you getting at?" Raylene sniffled. "Women do need men."

"Like we all need holes in our heads," Thelma replied defensively. "I don't need a man."

"Why not?"

"For starters, they think with their dicks, they don't communicate well, they have issues with monogamy, and to be quite honest, as long as there are floozies like Fe Henderson in the world, women like me are better off being single, because I'd end up going to jail behind bitches like her."

"Thelma."

"I'm just telling the truth."

"Not all men are that way. You do need a man. Don't you want kids and strong arms to hold you at night?"

Thelma pointed at Raylene. "What do I need strong arms holding me at night for when I'm trying to sleep?"

"What about kids and love and family?"

"I don't want any kids; I get plenty of love from my book club, church, and my family back home in Mississippi."

"Thelma, you know what I mean?" Raylene said. "Don't you want romance in your life?"

Thelma stopped. "Romance is fantasy. I say, cut the bullshit and keep it real. I am not interested in being a wife, mother, or girlfriend. Men serve one purpose for me, and one only, and I'm not ashamed to admit it. I wasn't put on this earth to please nobody but myself, and that's what I do. I get what I want, when I want it, on my own terms." Thelma grabbed her housecoat and disappeared into the bathroom.

Raylene got up so Thelma could have some time to herself and get ready.

Thelma and Raylene were the closest of the five book-club members, even though they were like night and day. Having grown up together and sharing more memories than the average set of best friends could shake a stick at, no matter how she felt, Thelma had Raylene's back.

GWENA HID BEHIND THE CAMERA on the set of the *Lamont Troy Show.*

"Don't panic," she told herself. Her voice was edged with tension, and she had licked her lips dry. "Stay calm, relax, and remember to breathe."

The atmosphere both inside and outside was alive with the buzz of chatter and energy. When she arrived, the protestors outside got in her face, hollered at her, and condemned her for being a part of what they were calling Marcus Brooks's conspiracy to sell bullshit to the public. Women of all ages, races, and pants sizes were marching in the heat, sweating for what they believed in, and Gwena couldn't blame them. If she wasn't in love with her job, and long over Marcus Brooks, she'd be out there too.

Inside was a different story. The mostly male audience waited attentively as producers, floor directors, and crew ran around like chickens in the dark, each trying to make sure his or her part was set for the show. It was a big day for the station; ratings were expected to be through the roof. Marcus's arrival had been publicized all week, and his appearance now was nothing short of eventful. Gwena found herself fatefully witnessing it all.

It had been twelve years since she'd seen Marcus, and now here he was less than twenty feet away, having his microphone run up the back of his shirt, around his collar, and to the inside of his jacket lapel. Gwena used her camera to zoom in on him, up close, without him knowing she was even in the same room. He looked the same: still tall, baby-faced, and pug-nosed. She also noticed that his top front teeth were now the same porcelain color and the same length. He was no longer the crooked-toothed outcast that she had dated in college.

Gwena wasn't worried about Marcus recognizing her, having long since graduated from her old wardrobe of tight pants, revealing tops, and short skirts. She was dressed way down in an over-size sweatshirt, loose-fitted blue jeans, prescription eyewear, and a baseball cap that hid her nest of raven-colored curls. She made sure Marcus wouldn't give her a second glance.

Seeing him brought back memories Gwena thought she was over, memories that made her insides shake, memories that now had her heart racing, her armpits damp with sweat, and her lips in desperate need of moisture.

Eva Rubio, the segment producer, blasted through the headphone mic from the control room. "Not enough headroom, camera two! If he goes on the air like that, he'll look like he's on *Fantasy Island* announcing the arrival of a damn plane! Zoom out!" She'd been hollering at people all morning.

Gwena adjusted the headroom in the camera's frame and centered Marcus on the monitor.

"That's better," Eva said. "Stay there coming out of commercial, and don't move unless I tell you to."

Silently, Gwena gave Eva the thumbs-up.

She watched Marcus case the studio, shielding his face from the overhead lights and ignoring Lamont Troy, who was trying to go over some of the questions with him. Instead, Marcus was too busy whistling at the few female crew members who didn't know any better than to wear ass-tight pants and nipple-revealing thin tops on a day like today. If they knew Marcus like Gwena did, they too would be dressed like baseball coaches with self-esteem issues. Yes, Marcus was still the same old Marcus.

The floor manager ran across the set with his hands up.

"Okay, everyone on your marks!" he barked the order. "We're up in ten . . . nine . . . eight . . ."

Gwena took a deep breath and steadied herself behind the camera. *Here we go. It will all be over soon.* She licked her lips again, wishing she'd brought some ChapStick, Carmex, Vaseline, Crisco . . . something!

"Five . . . four . . . three . . ."

The countdown was closing. Two seconds left before thirty-five markets met Marcus Brooks.

Lamont smiled into his designated camera and began the show.

Gwena shifted to steady her nerves as Eva's voice resounded in the headphones commanding orders, 101 things going on at once.

Finally, Lamont was introducing his special guest.

The all-male audience broke into loud applause and cheers.

"Camera two, you're on! Hold steady, give me some resistance on that angle." Eva's voice boomed in Gwena's ear.

Gwena clenched her hands around the grips, held the camera tight, avoided locking her knees, and remained steady.

Marcus looked into the camera as if it were his only audience. He profiled, sucked his teeth, and took his time holding everyone in broadcast limbo until he was ready to speak.

Finally, "What's up, Lamont?"

Lamont improvised a forced grin. It was the first time Gwena had ever seen the host look unsure about the order of things. He looked as if he'd gotten in over his head. She felt sorry for him, but it was too late. The show had to go on.

"Marcus, let's get right to business, shall we?" Lamont leafed through the cards. "You're here today to set the record straight about your latest book, correct?"

"I'm here to let everyone out there know that Marcus Brooks *is still a contender* and that my next book will be released regardless of a boycott, lack of a release date, and most recently, without an agent."

"You lost your agent?"

"Yeah, but he was a scrub anyway. I don't need him."

Lamont eyed Marcus with casual awe before continuing.

"Women from New York to California are protesting the release of your next book. Why?"

Marcus shrugged. The gesture was nonchalant. "I don't know, really. This book isn't any different than the others I've written."

"But isn't it true the title you've chosen for this one is *Bitches*?"

"That's right, Lamont, but so what? Women authors castrate men in novels every single day. Don't men have a right to fight back?"

More applause. Whistles.

Lamont sat back. "Is there a sense of competition between the sexes in fiction?"

"Sure there is. If it weren't, I wouldn't have hundreds of women outside this very building right now hating on me for nothing."

"But wasn't it women readers who initially made you success-ful? Don't you think that maybe they just feel slighted by their once-favorite author?"

"I was never interested in women reading my books. Of course, I'm grateful, but I don't owe them anything. I write for men, and now that men are reading my books, I feel more comfortable say-ing what I have to say using fiction as my vehicle of expression."

"You tell them, Marcus!" an audience member yelled. He waved a sign that read RELEASE BITCHES AND FREE MARCUS BROOKS!

A mixture of pity and discontent ran through Gwena. Marcus was pathetically trying to validate his own ignorance and arro-gance. She felt sorry for even knowing him, and for loving him at one time.

"Bitches." Lamont pondered the title and laughed as if he had nothing else to do. "Why that title?"

"Why not that title?" Marcus rubbed his hands together and rested them in his lap. "It's appropriate."

"And it's true that Pin Oak will not release the book until you change the title? Is that correct?"

"Don't believe everything you hear, Lamont."

"Does writing come easy for you?"

"Very. I can do it in my sleep."

Eva's voice blared in interruption. "Seven minutes to commercial."

Marcus shook his head. He seemed disappointed that Lamont wasn't reacting to his answers. "I couldn't have been more deliberate with this book. It's about women that men can't trust, women that men can't stand, women that get on men's nerves. The book is about bitches."

"What if the book doesn't release?"

"That won't happen. If I have to put it out myself, then I will." Marcus huffed. "Now, let's talk about something else."

"Okay." Lamont got comfortable. He put the cards down. "Several years ago, you were quoted by the *Atlanta Journal-Constitution* as saying, and I quote, 'I don't give a damn that women read my books. Women are God's personal misdemeanor.' This after the sale of your first book was to over eighty percent women readers." Lamont looked at Marcus. "Did you say that?"

"I don't recall those exact words, but if you have it in print, then I won't deny it," Marcus said. "It sounds like it was taken out of context. You know the press is foul. For all I know, Jayson Blair could have had something to do with mixing my words up."

The audience laughed.

Gwena read it for what it was. Marcus was avoiding the questions.

"This guy is taciturn," Eva said before sending out her next order. "Camera five, give me full shot."

The summer intern operating camera five was Lance Harris, Latice's son. He wasn't paying attention, too busy listening to Marcus, awed at the author's uncompromising attitude.

Gwena noticed immediately. She tried to get his attention, but it was too late.

Eva was already barking into the headphones. "Dammit, camera five, do you hear me! I need a full shot, for crying out loud!"

Lance startled to attention, did as he was told, but it was obvious he didn't appreciate being yelled at.

So much was going on behind the scenes.

Gwena wondered how many more minutes were remaining as she continued watching.

Lamont continued. "How necessary is it to write a book called *Bitches* when relationships between men and women, particularly of color, are in a state of emergency?"

Again, Marcus took his time answering. "The only reason relationships are in a state of emergency is because women no longer want to play the roles meant for them. It has nothing to do with men or my book."

"Do you really believe that?"

"Of course. It's the truth," Marcus said. "At the very core of their beings, all women are after three things, which I call the three D's: diamonds, dick, and dough."

"Edit!" Eve yelled, but it was too late. The expletive had gone live.

Marcus shifted, sucked his teeth, and drove his point home. "It's like this—women want to be spoiled, pampered, and waited on by us, but what do we get?" Marcus sat quietly, waiting for the host to give him an answer.

Lamont was perplexed. "I don't know."

"Not a fucking thing, that's what!" Marcus told him.

"Edit!" Eva yelled from the control room. Again, it was too late.

Marcus was on a roll. "It's time to start being real, draw the line down the middle, and give women the same shit they dish out."

Now Eva was in the control room using her own obscene language.

Lamont thought for a moment and shook his head as if Marcus's words were fantasy. "Fifty-fifty?"

"Yeah," Marcus chimed in. "That's why I have no sympathy

for women, because they fake this perfect portrait of who they think they are, but in reality, women can't figure themselves out, so why should men? Women are a bunch of————who fake being difficult."

This time Eva and the control-room edit crew caught the derogatory language coming out of Marcus's mouth.

Gwena could hear the producer applauding the one bad word they were able to catch.

"Is the name-calling necessary?"

"Yes," Marcus said. "We thought all this time a woman's mouth was for running when in fact it's for————."

Eva could be seen angrily flailing her arms in the air, sending the production notes raining down on everyone in there with her.

Gwena was the only nonreactive woman in the entire room. Marcus was good at shocking the shit out of even the most suspecting person, and she knew this.

"What kind of brother are you?" Lamont sat back as if Marcus had threatened to kill the president and tried to bring him in on the job.

"I'm reasonable, intelligent, was raised in a good home by a loving woman who is now in Heaven, and I'm personally concerned about liberating men from the stigma that we don't read fiction. Aside from that, I'm fun to be around."

"What do the women in your family have to say about your attitude?"

"My mother is deceased. Before her, there were no other women. She taught me the evil ways of women and how manipulative they can be. I'm sure she's looking down on me with pride and admiration, that's all that matters to me."

"What was the most important thing she taught you?"

"Do unto others as they do unto you."

Lamont leaned back and laughed haughtily as he looked into the camera. "Do you think the boycott is karma for the first two books? Are you somehow getting what you deserve?"

"I don't believe in karma. Karma is for weak people who don't believe in what they do or say. How can I be punished for believing in myself?"

"So, you're not worried?"

"No. I'm not going to let the opinions of a few skeezers with books and of critics with too much time on their hands validate me."

"Interesting," Lamont said. It seemed to be the only comment he could muster.

Gwena caught the look of irritation Lamont shot to the control room. Time seemed to be moving in slow motion for them all.

"Okay, everyone, be ready," Eva said again as Marcus continued to lay out his view on things.

"That's why I have no sympathy for the women outside boycotting me. If I were some pretty mofo like Travis Hunter or E. Lynn Harris, this would not be an issue, but because I go against the grain and try to give people something a little different, I'm being nailed to a cross."

"Do you feel crucified?"

"No."

"Do you feel alienated by other male authors in your genre?"

"I'm an original, designed by God, and nobody can alienate me. I don't consider myself in line with them. Marcus Brooks is in a class by himself."

"Is it about the money?"

"Of course it's about the money, but at the same time, it's about the message in the books. I have something to say."

Finally, the floor director motioned his hand in an upward circular gesture. A commercial break was coming.

Lamont had to hold his hand up. "Before we go into commercial, let me ask you this." Lamont leaned in and eyed Marcus. He scanned him. It was the questioning style that he was famous for. "Who is the bitch in your life?"

Marcus laughed. "What do you mean?"

"Well, it's true that all fiction is not all fiction, right?"

"I suppose."

"Then who was your point of reference for this book? Is it someone you know?"

The air was still. Marcus looked like a ghost had slid up his spine. "Well . . . I'll tell you like this. She used to be special. She was a girl I knew in college. I thought she was the one, but she turned out to be nothing but an open can of worms."

Lamont let the remark stand. "We'll be right back with more from controversial author Marcus Brooks, after a word from our sponsors," Lamont said.

Off the air, the audience went wild.

"Marcus! Marcus! Marcus!" men chanted. Every call of his name sounded like a death knell to Gwena's ears. It was too much. She locked her camera down and waited for the break to be over.

Starvette Gilliam, the handheld-camera op, put her camera down in quiet protest and walked out of the studio, making it obvious that at least one person on the crew had heard and seen enough.

Lance backed away from a nearby overhead mic and pumped his fist in silent support of the author.

Gwena rolled her eyes. Seven years of therapy had unhinged her from anger and personal guilt. Watching Marcus now, she felt nothing. Her nervousness had dissipated.

However, she did realize that nothing had changed. Marcus was still arrogant, loud, confrontational, and pretentious, just like the woman who taught him everything he knew, his mama, Junesta Brooks—a consummate mess starter, God rest her evil soul.

She saw Eva pop two aspirin, gulp down a glass of water, and head toward the studio—a sign more shit was about to hit the fan.

Eva charged into the room, her heels clicking militantly against the concrete floor. "Mr. Brooks, do you mind toning the language down? This is *not* cable."

"I'm exercising free speech," Marcus blared across the room. "You have an editor, don't you?"

"Yes, but it would be beneficial to all of us if you remained conscious of where you are. This is a public affiliate."

"I know where I'm at," Marcus shot back. He checked Eva out from head to toe, and in spite of the large wedding ring she wore, he said, "Agree to have dinner with me later tonight, and I'll consider it."

"Negro, please. So you can call me a bitch while I'm eating or something crazy like that?" Eva snapped back. "I don't think so."

Gwena laughed at that one. Eva was sharp, but Gwena had known Marcus longer, and unless Eva's forty-five years were as deep as Marcus's thirty-two, the driven producer was about to get told.

Marcus was ready to show his true colors. "I'm going to call you a bitch whether you sleep with me or not, bitch!"

Lamont Troy stepped in. "Marcus, you can't just say what you want if you plan on getting through this interview," he said in a weak effort to break the ice, but the time for that had passed.

Eva was already red in the face and looking at the author with venom in her eyes. "I want you out of my studio, right now!" she yelled. Then she called out an order to the host. "Tom, call in the backup guest."

"Trying to keep a brother down," Lance said. "Let the man have his hour."

The men in the audience began to boo and hiss. Some walked out.

"Mr. Harris, get back to your camera!" Eva yelled. Then she looked around at the rest of the crew. "Everyone back to your positions!"

The boy sucked his teeth at his scolding, but obeyed.

Marcus stood and yelled across the room. "Lamont, get a goddamned backbone! This is your show." Then he pointed at Eva. "And you need to get back into that control room and do what you are paid to do, instead of trying to censor me."

Eva took off her shoe and threw it at Marcus. The closed-toed black leather strap-around grazed his ear.

Marcus checked for blood. "What's your fucking problem?"

Marcus stood up and snatched off his lapel mic, removed his shoe, aimed, and hit Eva on the forehead with his size 10.

She reeled back on her feet as a red mark shaped like part of Marcus's shoe heel appeared. Angered, Eva made her move across the studio floor toward the step leading to the set and charged at Marcus.

Gwena removed her headphones, but hesitated. As much as she wanted to help break up the fight, her common sense told her it would only make things worse if Marcus recognized her.

Luckily, two of the male crew members intervened and kept the combatants separated. Eva had to be dragged back into the control room as she yelled obscenities at Marcus.

"I didn't want to do this pothole of a show anyway!" The author moved across the studio, grabbed his shoe and satchel, and made a beeline to the exit.

"I'm pressing charges, you bastard!" Eva screamed.

When he walked by Gwena, she turned her back to him and held her head down. Marcus stopped long enough to check her out from behind. Then he slapped her on the ass and walked out. Gwena gasped but remained incognito.

Lance ran over to Gwena. "Why'd you let him do that to you?"

"Men like that only want trouble, and I don't have time for that kind of drama," Gwena lied. Secretly, she wanted to hurt Marcus, but she had to be an example to her friend's son. Instead, she advised the boy, "And what were you thinking when you boldly tried to defend that man's ignorance in front of Eva?"

Lance shrugged. "I was feeling what Mr. Brooks was saying."

"Feeling it?" Gwena quizzed. "He was terrible to Eva."

"I know girls who act just like Mrs. Rubio. Stuck up, bossy, and always trying to tell people what to do. Besides, she threw her shoe at him," Lance said, as if that made his point stronger. "He had a right to hit her with his shoe. It's equality across the board, just like Mr. Brooks said. Fifty-fifty."

Gwena pulled the boy by his shirt out of earshot from the others. "Lance Harris, if your mother heard you, she'd beat *you* with a shoe."

Lance stuck his chest out. "I'm seventeen. I have my own mind. My mama can't run me anymore. Besides, Marcus is right."

"And what makes you such an authority?" Gwena asked.

"I'm around females all day, so I know."

"Know what?"

"About the three M's."

Gwena picked up on Marcus's influence on the young man. "What are the three M's?"

"Money, marriage, and me," Lance boasted. "And the only reason girls from school are interested in me is because I'm captain of the basketball team and I'm probably going to end up playing pro somewhere."

"Is Christy that way?" Gwena asked, referring to Lance's current love interest and Mount Zephaniah church member.

He looked distracted. "Christy?" He shook his head. "Christy's cool for right now, but she's not my type of girl—no disrespect."

"None taken." Gwena walked back over to her camera.

When the show resumed, Lamont was introducing Jessie James, the male stripper who was running for mayor of Dallas.

After the taping, Gwena headed to the break room to call Latice. If anyone was going to get Lance straight, it was his mother. Afterwards, Gwena headed home, glad that she was out of the studio and away from Marcus Brooks. As far as she was concerned, if she never saw him again, it would be too soon.

LATICE WATCHED LANCE walk out of the television station toward the car. It was after five, and the boycotters were gone. Downtown was emptying out.

She watched him, her son and only seed. Fourteen hours of labor to produce him at a healthy seven pounds ten ounces. She still remembered waiting too late to get to the hospital, which resulted in her having to deliver him naturally. He was the first and only man to split her taint and still manage to be the absolute love of her life.

Lance was tall, slim, pimple free, and two notches more handsome than his father was at the same age. It had been a struggle raising him while a single parent, but Latice had managed to see Lance through without serious incident and without his father's help.

When Lance got into the car, he kissed his mother on the cheek. "Hey, beautiful." He smiled. "How was work?"

Latice softened. "Work was work."

She felt his eyes on her. "You look upset—what's the matter?" he asked.

"I'd be better if my son told me why he mouthed off at his boss today." She put the car in drive and pulled into traffic. "Gwena called me."

"Then why do I need to tell you?"

Latice closed the sunroof and turned on the air. "I want to hear your version."

Lance's face was devoid of emotion. "Mrs. Rubio yelled at me."

"For what?"

"I wasn't paying attention, but—"

"Have that attitude when you are out of college and living on your own. Don't do it while I'm still paying your way in this world."

"What happened to me telling my side?"

"You admitted to not paying attention—what else is there for you to say?"

"But she yelled at me."

"Lance."

"Okay, okay, Ma."

"Don't 'okay, okay' me," Latice said. "When you turn eighteen, then you can be the man you want to be, but this internship is just as important as basketball, and I'm not going to sit by and let you mess it up. Got it?"

"Got it." Lance's response was dry. "I hear you."

Latice considered herself a fair judge—as a parole officer she was accustomed to hearing both sides of a story.

Lance laughed through his broad smile. "Did Ms. Phelps tell you that Marcus Brooks hit Eva with a shoe?"

"No. I take it you find it funny?"

"She deserved it. She hit him first." Then Lance broke loose as if he were at a comedy show. "It was a perfect shot. I've never seen anything like it."

"Lance, that's not funny. Was she hurt?"

"I don't know," he answered absently. "But she had a mark on her forehead."

"What if this had happened to me instead of Eva? Then would you think that?"

Lance kept his eyes front and center. "You're my mother, which makes it different. If it were you, Marcus Brooks would be in the hospital right now."

Latice admired her son's protective nature, but she refrained from letting him read it on her face. There was still a bigger resolve to get to. "Men should treat women with respect at all times, no matter what. I'm not different from Eva, understood?"

"But why?" Lance argued. "Women don't always respect men."

"That's beside the point. Men should not hit women."

"Mom, I know you mean well, but I'm with Mr. Brooks on this one. I'm not even a pro basketball star yet, and women are trying to sleep with me, just like he said. Why should I call a bitch a queen when she's actually a bitch?"

"Watch your mouth!"

Lance shook his head. "Even if a female is throwing herself at me like they do all the time?"

"Son, I don't care if you come home and she's butt-naked in your bed. It's your responsibility to make that woman put on her clothes and engage in some conversation, because she's a woman who probably needs to be treated better than she treats herself." Latice turned a corner and checked her rearview mirror. It was time to get her microbraids touched up, and her eyebrows needed arching. She made a mental note to call her stylist in the morning.

"Do you believe all people were created equal like Dr. King preached?" Lance asked.

"Of course I do, honey." Latice smiled. She loved it when her son made intelligent references. It showed her that putting him through private school was worth it.

"Well, Marcus Brooks thinks the same. His philosophy is that we are all equal and men should treat women equal."

"Hitting a woman with a shoe is not treating her equal," Latice contested.

"It is if she threw her shoe first. Don't that make it self-defense?"

"Enough." Latice pulled onto the freeway and headed south toward Oakcliff. "You will always do the right thing like *I* taught you and not some infantile author who didn't carry you for nine months." Latice turned on the radio. An old Teddy Pendergrass tune blared through the speakers. The song took her back—1980 was a good year. She was married then and could still fit into a size 8.

Lance reached over and turned off the radio. "Where do you draw the line, Mom?"

Latice put her concentration back on the road as she slid into the middle lane and pushed the speedometer five miles over the limit. Her mini-flashback to a time before Teddy Pendergrass was in a wheelchair gone instantly. It was funny how time flew. "I'm sorry, son, what were you saying?"

"The line?" he said again. "When do you *not* do the right thing? Where is your point of resistance? Everybody has one."

"Son, you should always do what's right. There is no point of resistance for me. Getting fed up when you have a son to raise is not an option for women like me. I always ask myself, what would Jesus do?"

"Jesus was a man, right?" Lance quizzed her.

"Right."

"I'm a man, right?"

Latice was uncomfortable answering this question. Indeed, Lance was seventeen, no longer wetting the bed or needing her to change his diaper, but he was still her baby. She took a quick glance at him and smiled. "Right."

"And Dad is a man, right?"

"Not much of one, but yes, Rodrick is a man."

"I hate it when you do that," Lance said.

"Do what?"

"Say bad things about Dad. You're always dissing him." Lance stared outside the passenger window.

"I can't help it. Your father abandoned us." Latice slowed her pace as she weaved in and out of traffic. "And that heffa, Angela, he's married to isn't even out of her first year of college. No girl that age knows anything about a forty-two-year-old man."

"But Dad is a man, just like Jesus, which goes back to my point."

"Okay, make your point." She'd become angry just thinking

about her ex and that skinny, short, green-eyed dummy he was with.

"My point is women and men are *different*. Men think different, so when you ask me what would Jesus do, my answer is going to be different from your answer because I'm a man."

"But it should be a higher difference, like turning the other cheek or refusing to hit someone just because they hit you. Doing what's right has nothing to do with what sex you are."

"Would you hit a man out of anger?"

Latice thought for a moment and then for the sake of serving as a good role model for her son, she told her truth. "No. I let the Lord fight my battles."

She exited the freeway. Then, as if in afterthought, Latice apologized. "I'm sorry for talking about your father," she said. "But I'm still angry, and I have to get it out sometimes."

"I know." Lance smiled at his mother. "Thanks, and if I ever see Angela on the street by herself, I'm going to bitch-slap that ho."

Fortunately, they were pulled into the driveway and the car was in park; otherwise, Latice was sure she would have driven straight into her kitchen. "Lance Eric Harris! What has gotten into you?"

"Marcus Brooks said—"

"No more talk about Marcus Brooks! I'm sick of hearing his name." Hollering was something Latice rarely had to do with Lance, but every now and then, she had to go there and check him in her *mother's only* tone.

Lance looked disappointed and misunderstood. "But I'm supposed to be able to express myself to you, right?"

Latice gave her son a look of certainty. "Yes, but not about Marcus Brooks." She removed the keys from the ignition. "Just go in the house and wash the dishes so I can cook."

Lance bounced his head on the headrest out of aggravation. "I hate it when you do that to me," he complained.

"Do what?" Latice gathered her things and was one foot out of the car.

"Leave me with no alternative."

"I always leave you with an alternative." Latice scooted to the edge of the seat as she listened.

Lance looked at her. "If *I* don't wash the dishes, *I* don't eat. That's some *alternative*."

Latice frowned. "You got some selfish nerve to think you're the only hungry person around here," she snapped. "Cooking is just as tedious as having to wash dishes." She bounded out of the car and marched inside. "Now go."

She hated being at odds with her son, but sometimes he was selfish, like his father, and that selfishness pissed her off when it surfaced. She wanted desperately to break Lance of his father's ways but knew that genetics had her beat. He would have to learn the repercussions of that kind of behavior on his own.

❧

The light on the answering machine was blinking. Latice put her things on the table and checked the messages.

Lance dragged himself from the kitchen to his room. It was obvious that he was upset at the scolding.

Latice ignored him and listened to the messages. The first was from Naomi. *He'll get over it. He always does,* she told herself.

"Hey, Tice, it's Nay. I was wondering if I could ride with you to the concert."

Click!

Latice had forgotten all about the concert. She hadn't even picked out an outfit. She hoped her black wrap dress was clean.

Beep!

"Latice, this is Thelma. Raylene is with me, so don't worry about having to pick her up for the concert tonight. Just meet us at the Gypsy around eight thirty."

Click!

Latice checked the clock on the wall. It was already six fifteen. She needed to put a move on it.

Beep!

"Sister Harris, this is Reverend Robinson. The reason I'm calling is that I'm trying to get in touch with Raylene, and I know the book club is meeting tonight. Could you please have her call me? I'd appreciate it. Have a good evening."

Click!

Nope.

Delete.

Beep!

"Hey, Lance, it's your father. I was calling to see how you were doing. Tell your mama I said hello. Call me, son."

Click!

Latice sneered and pressed the SAVE button only for the sake of her son. Rodrick didn't even have the decency to leave a return phone number, which he knew they didn't have. Rodrick Harris was an asshole, and that was the truth. Latice wondered over and over why and how she could ever have allowed such a fool to pollinate her flower.

Beep!

"Hey, Lance, this is Christy. I was calling to see if you wanted to go check out the new Taye Diggs and Samuel Jackson movie. I can come by and pick you up if you need me to. Call me."

Latice liked Christy and thought she'd make a good future wife for her son. She was a nice, smart, God-fearing girl, and as cute as she wanted to be. The grandbabies would be anointed with good looks if Lance stopped trying to be a player like his father and settled down.

The farther she could keep the gold diggers away from her son, the better. She lost Rodrick to one, and she wasn't about to lose her son to one as well. All bets were on Christy.

After the machine recued, Latice headed upstairs to change out of her work clothes. The day had been long, and some good music featuring D'Angelo and drinks with her girls was just what she needed. Marcus Brooks, without even knowing her, had almost ruined her day. If it was up to her, she'd put the man under the jail and throw away the key.

Naomi strutted down the hall as she brushed her hair back and put it in a ponytail. It had been a long and eventful day at the salon. Three of her customers had protested earlier, and the entire place was lit with the gossip about Marcus Brooks hitting the segment producer with a shoe.

By the end of her workday, she had just enough time to come home, call Latice to bum a ride, shower, and change. It was after eight when she finally emerged from the room dressed and ready to go.

She sat on the couch next to her husband. "What time are you leaving?"

"We go on last. I'm going to watch this and then head out." Vincent put his arm around her. He was dressed casually in a fitted T-shirt, jeans, and a pair of black All-Star Converse sneakers.

Naomi tuned in to what he was watching on the television. "What is this?" she asked.

"It's the *Lamont Troy Show*. I didn't want to miss it, so I recorded it."

Maybe Vincent's television habits need to be monitored. "For what?" Naomi quizzed sarcastically. "I heard about what he did. Why would you want to see *that* garbage again?"

"It's not garbage." Vincent released a sigh. "You haven't even seen the entire interview, Naomi," he replied flatly. "Stop being so quick to judge."

"I don't need to see the entire interview to know it's crap," she snapped smartly and loud enough to make sure Vincent could hear her over the television's volume. "I read his first two books and wasn't impressed." Naomi was up on her reading, and rightly so.

"Well, lucky for Marcus you aren't his target audience." Vincent played in her hair, then leaned over and kissed her on the forehead.

"Don't do that."

"Do what?"

"Try and pacify what I'm saying with a kiss."

"I'm not trying to pacify you."

"Aren't you going to turn this off? I don't think you should be watching it."

"It's just television."

"Vince, everything you watch has an effect on you, and Marcus Brooks is no exception to the rule."

Vincent removed his arm from around Naomi and held her hand instead. "Why are you hating on this man? You don't even know him."

"I know enough." Naomi pushed his hand away. "He's a narcissist, and he hates women. Don't you have a problem with that?"

"I don't hate women." Vincent scratched his growing beard. "To each his own."

"Let me remind you that in his first book, he wrote about two men who take advantage of a woman, and she ends up killing herself."

Vincent shook his head. "The men in *Two Birds One Stoned* felt bad about what happened," Vincent said in the author's defense. "And don't forget, they wouldn't have done it had the woman not lied about who she was in the first place. I always have to remind you of that."

Naomi snuggled into her husband as she used her index finger on his thigh to drive in her point of view. "We have sons, and I'm not going to have them growing up hating women for no reason at all. Speaking of which, have you talked to your father lately?" She reached over, grabbed the remote from the table, and muted the television.

Vince's head fell back in resignation. "I was watching that, Nay." He looked like a moviegoer who had been disturbed by the annoying ring of a cell phone, but Naomi didn't care. She wanted to talk.

"It's a tape. You can rewind it when I leave. I'm trying to talk to you." She tossed the remote out of arm's reach. "Have you?"

"No. I'll try and call him later."

"You said that last time. How long are you going to let him go on like he is? You need to say something, Vince."

"Actually, no, I don't, which is what I've been trying to tell you. My old man has been Muslim since I can remember, and my mother doesn't seem to mind."

"Then why tell me you're going to call when you're not?"

"I never said I was. You are the one who wants me to call."

"So, his grabbing your mother by the arm and literally dragging her away from the boys' birthday party a month ago doesn't bother you?"

"No. He'd been asking her to go for over an hour. My mother is social; my father is not. Sometimes he has to pull her out of a room—otherwise they'd be there all night with her yapping and him sitting there grumpy and mad."

"Does he hit her as well?"

"Nay, you're going too far. You need to back off my family."

Naomi let up. "Okay, fine, Vince, but I think as a man and as his son who loves him, you need to check your father." She looked at her watch. "And until you do, I don't think I want any of our children around him." She looked over her shoulder in hopes that Latice would be pulling into the drive.

Vincent got up and without saying a word retrieved the remote and sat back down on the couch, away from his wife.

Naomi spoke up, changing the subject to keep her husband's attention on her and not on Lamont Troy or Marcus Brooks.

"Did I tell you Lance already has scouts coming to his school? Latice is proud of him."

"Which schools?"

"So far UT, Arizona, Duke, and I believe she said Howard."

"Good schools, all of 'em."

Vincent knew basketball. He'd played in college on a scholarship until he met Naomi and they became pregnant. As soon as she found out, Naomi demanded Vincent choose between her and sports, so he did. He dropped out and took to his second-favorite pastime, which was music. Now, he made his money as a professional guitarist. When he wasn't on the road touring as a backup musician, Vincent Hargrove was at home spending time with his wife and children. He was no longer concerned with the remote control. "That kid is going places if he doesn't mess up his life."

Naomi sighed. "Vince, everybody's not you."

"That's true," he replied with a sense of absence. "But he still has to take care of himself."

Naomi rolled her eyes. "Lance is smart. He won't go sticking his penis into any and everything walking by. Babies and baby mama drama won't ruin his career."

Vincent scratched his brow. "I was actually talking about the boy getting injured. I chose to stop playing ball because I loved my children and my wife. It had nothing to do with the drama."

"You know what?" Naomi blurted out, not minding Vincent's comment. "I hear what you're saying, but the bottom line is that Lance is not you, and I'm sure *his* girlfriend will never have to worry about another woman coming up pregnant at the same time she is. His mother has him on lock."

"He's still a man who at some point has to make his own decisions. Latice can't be there with him forever. It's deeper than that. Men need space."

"Like Kobe Bryant, I guess."

"The man apologized for his mistake. Damn."

"So, that don't make what he did forgivable."

"*We* don't know what he did, Nay," Vincent said defensively. "*We* weren't there."

"No, that's not it." Naomi was irritated by Vincent's flippant behavior. "Common sense isn't buried at the center of the earth. It's not that deep. If men would just *think* before they acted, *we* wouldn't be having this conversation."

She scooted back over to her husband's side, regardless of his wanting her at a distance. They were husband and wife, and whenever Vincent acted like he didn't want to be around her, she showed him what a wife was supposed to do with her husband by sticking closer to him.

"And another thing," he objected. "I wish you wouldn't get on the phone with your friends and tell our business."

"Explain yourself." Naomi sat up as if on guard.

"The other night I heard you tell Latice about the argument we had," Vince said. "That needs to stay behind closed doors."

"I had to tell somebody. My feelings were hurt."

"Then what am I here for? You never told me your feelings were hurt."

"That's because you were the cause."

Naomi sat up, grabbed the remote, and turned off the television. "You know what? If I wasn't married to you and the mother of your sons, maybe I could have the luxury of always thinking about myself, not deal with my family issues, have children by two different men, and jack off to Lamont Troy during my off time. I wouldn't think of us in terms of me and you. But I don't have that luxury. I'm a grown-ass woman who has responsibilities like children to think about."

"What is that supposed to mean?" His eyes searched hers.

"I just call it like it is. That's what it means."

"No, you call it like you see it." Vincent reached over and

grabbed the remote. His face remained calm as he channel surfed. "I never thought I'd say this, but Marcus Brooks said something today that I actually agreed with."

"Please don't go there." Naomi stared at her husband, daring him to say something she wasn't going to like.

"He said men should stop being afraid to be men and just do and say what comes natural."

"And what does that have to do with us?"

"I'm going to start treating you exactly how you treat me. I'm tired of holding back." Vincent shook his head. "And I've been too quiet for too long. I'm sick of you riding me all the time about me being me."

Silence split the couple.

"Great, my husband is quoting a man who throws shoes at women. Vincent, you're a man—act like one and realize the shit that Marcus Brooks is spitting will only make things worse between you and your *wife*."

Vince held his hands up in submission. "I'm not in the mood for your commentary or self-righteous bickering today. It's bad enough you put our business out in the street with Latice, then you throw my mistakes up in my face, and that bull has been over eight years. Now you wanna come in here, interrupt my time to myself by throwing a fucking fit over nothing." Vince leaned back. "I'm sick of it."

"And I'm sick of coming home every day to your ass sitting up in this house like you don't have shit to do. We have kids, one of which is not mine and only comes during the summer, thanks to you."

"We agreed that I would stay home with the kids in the summer when I'm home. I'm here, so what's the problem?"

"That's all you are, Vince, is here. You don't take them out. You sit up in here for days on end with the same clothes on. You don't feed them healthy food, and you don't make them brush their teeth. It's like you don't care."

"Why can't I just care differently because I'm a man? This is summer, school's out, and I don't think there is anything wrong with me and my kids walking around the house in yesterday's clothes, letting our nuts and flat chests hang while cooling out for a few measly hot summer days."

"And when it's time for you to go back on tour, I'll have to reprogram the boys, which will be right around the time school starts. Do you know how hard it is to get twins up and dressed when they've been programmed to be up all night?"

"Why does everything always have to be to your time frame and to your schedule?"

"Because I'm with the boys more than you are. That's two personalities I have to deal with every day, and it would be nice if you could just come home and fit in, instead of changing things."

"Three months is all I have to split between the twins, Sierra, and you. It's the only time I have to bond. For me, it's about creating memorable moments with my kids and with you."

"Then put them to bed on time, make them bathe, take them to the goddamned zoo instead of being holed up in the house all day. That would be memorable for me!"

She waited for her husband to respond, but Vincent never moved from the couch or said anything in rebuttal. Instead, he flipped the VCR back to PLAY and upped the volume on the television, tuning her out.

She shrugged her shoulders in an I-don't-give-a-damn fashion, got up, and retreated to the back. The last thing she was worried about was Vincent losing focus because some fool on television had him thinking he could just do what he wanted around her and the boys. She wasn't having it, and Vince had better get himself together or else she was going to suggest they seek counseling. Naomi waited in the bedroom until she heard Latice's car horn outside. The television had been turned off and Vincent had made his exodus without telling her, and it pissed her off more than it hurt, but that was her husband and she allowed him the right to get upset. Married couples disagreed sometimes, but Naomi knew, no matter what, that she and Vincent would always be together.

Raylene had been hiding at Thelma's all week, refusing to answer Will's calls to her cell and skipping all her weekly church activities, Bible study, prayer meeting, usher board meeting, and women's auxiliary prayer meeting to avoid him.

When the doorbell rang, she was in the den listening to music and writing in her journal.

"Raylene, could you get that?" Thelma yelled from the back. "I'm still not dressed."

Raylene didn't mind until she opened the door and saw Will standing there, his eyes hidden behind shades. He carried flowers and a small box.

She talked to him through the screen. "What are you doing here?"

"I've come to see you."

"How did you find me?"

"I saw your car." Will removed the shades. "We need to talk."

"There's nothing to talk about." Raylene folded her arms in front of her to hide her trembling hands.

Will held the flowers out in truce. "Can I at least come in?"

He knew she had a weakness for flowers. These were forget-me-nots. Raylene thought for a few seconds, then opened the door, and stepped aside. *What am I doing?*

Will leaned over in passing and landed a kiss on her cheek as he walked by and handed her the flowers. She could have done without the kiss, but the flowers were too adorable to deny. She carried them with her into the den, smelling the petals. Will scoped out the place while she lowered the volume on the radio.

Finally, he made himself comfortable on the couch. "I like how Sister Wade has this place laid out."

"I did most of it," Raylene said. "Thelma likes a relaxed environment that blends the outdoors with the indoors."

"What do you call it?"

"Feng shui. It's centuries old."

"You've outdone yourself. I can't wait to see what you do with our home."

Raylene stood silent. She hadn't even though about returning to the house. She still hadn't found the courage to leave Thelma's.

Will continued to look around as the music played in the background. Raylene felt like she was on a bad date. Then he asked. "That's not Yolanda Adams, is it?"

"No," she huffed. "It's not church music."

"You too good for gospel music now?"

"It's Lauryn Hill," Raylene said. "Not Satan." She walked over and turned off the CD player. The room filled with a silence so thick, Raylene had to clear her throat in an effort to shatter the awkwardness.

Will patted the couch. "Come sit."

"I'd rather stand."

She didn't want to put herself in a vulnerable position. She still was very much in love with Will and knew it was going to take a generous amount of effort to get to the bottom of what had happened last Sunday. She had to keep her distance.

Monroe came in wagging his tail.

She watched Will greet the dog, pet him, and act as if they were old friends. Monroe hung around long enough to get what little attention he could and then bounded away to another part of the house.

She felt Will's eyes back on her.

"You look gorgeous. Is that a new outfit?"

"Sort of."

Raylene knew she was looking good. She'd put extra effort into her outfit for the evening. She wanted to look sexy for the concert, and Will's recognition got high marks with her ego. Unfortunately, he didn't remember buying the outfit for her on her last birthday.

She looked at her watch.

"Are you going somewhere?"

"Tonight is book-club night."

"Oh, yeah."

"Will, what do you want?"

"I want you to come back home so we can put this behind us and move forward."

"It's that simple for you, isn't it?" Raylene felt a rush of anger rise in her. "Every time I look at you or think about you, all I can see is you standing there with Felicia Henderson's mouth wrapped around your . . ." The word lodged in her throat.

"Baby, it meant nothing."

"Obviously not to you, but it meant something to me."

She watched him ponder and then shrug. "I'd forgive you."

He's lying. "Will, you need to go."

Raylene moved toward the door.

"Wait," Will said. "I have something for you." He handed her a royal-blue velvet jewelry box. The kind rings came in.

"What's this?"

"Open it and see."

Raylene held the box for a few seconds. She'd been strong up until now, but the truth was she was a sucker for a good gift. She peeled the box open. There, nestled in a cushion, was a two-carat ring with platinum encasing. The ring took her breath. "Will . . ." She took the ring out and put it on her finger. "It's beautiful."

He stood to his feet and walked over to her. "It's yours, from me to you. Ray, I'm sorry, and if there is anything I can do to make it up to you, then I will." He smiled and gently swiped the bangs of hair from her eyes.

Now, Raylene sat. This was what she meant when she told
Thelma about being wooed. She thought about accepting Will's
apology, but making him suffer for a little while had great returns.
The ring had to cost him at least $1,400.

He sat back down like a man who'd won the lottery. "How
was your week?" he asked.

Raylene thought for a moment. "Fine. Long. I barely got any
work done with everything that's been going on around here."

"Did you see the news? The police are looking for that author,
Marcus Brooks."

Raylene's hypnotized stare on the ring broke. "For what?"

"He supposedly assaulted the producer over at Fox."

That was news to Raylene. She hadn't watched television
today and wasn't up on the happenings.

"Over two hundred women showed up to protest. Did you go?"

Raylene nodded. "I was supposed to go, but I don't like Marcus Brooks, I don't read his books, and I couldn't care less that he
was in town. Not to mention, I overslept." She studied the ring on
her finger again.

"You like it?"

Raylene removed the ring from her finger and gave it back.
"Yes, but I'm still hurting, and it's not going to fix what's wrong
between us. I can't take it."

"I gave it to you." He tried to give it back. "It's yours."

"I don't want it." She stood to her feet. "Will, you need to
leave."

"Baby, tell me what you want. How can I fix this?"

"I don't know. I don't even know if you can. That's why I'm
here thinking about it."

"But . . . I told you I was sorry."

"Yes, you are sorry. A sorry man of God."

"I'm human."

"Yes, I know that," Raylene said. Her voice cracked, and the
heat of tears welled inside her.

Will made his move. "I'll do whatever it takes to make this right."

The tears fell. Raylene quickly mopped them with the back of her hand. "I want to know why. Why did you do it?"

Somewhere in the house, Monroe's chain could be heard, which meant he was moving about.

Will shrugged. "I don't know. I was weak in the flesh, and Sister Henderson just kept making herself available." He let out a long sigh. "To be honest, I did it because I felt like you weren't there for me."

"Excuse me?" Raylene was thrown.

"I don't know. It was as if you didn't care one way or the other what I did. It was no secret to anyone that Sister Henderson was after me. The whole church knew."

"So it's my fault?"

"I'm not saying that."

"Then what are you saying, Will, because I'm failing to understand."

He threw up his hands, not wanting to argue. "As your man, I have a need to feel protected just like you do. Sometimes, I would like to see you show genuine concern for having me to yourself. If another woman is trying to step to me and I'm doing my thing and can't put her in her place, it would be nice to know that you did it for me."

"That's not my job."

"See, I don't get it." Will stood up. "If any man stepped to you and was out of line while I was around, you'd want me to say something, right?"

"That's what you're supposed to do." Raylene felt herself getting more upset. She didn't appreciate being blamed for actions that were not her own.

"Then why can't it be both ways? I've seen Felicia disrespect you on more that one occasion, and you've done absolutely nothing."

"First of all, that skank didn't disrespect me. How dare you try to make it seem as if I inadvertently put your dick in her mouth."

"I didn't say that, but you can't deny I'm right."

Her tone went up two octaves as she wagged her finger in his face. "You are not right! Felicia Henderson had no interest in me. She wasn't trying to have sex with me! It was you she was after. You! You! You!"

Will remained seated. "Even at the church anniversary you left us together in my study after she'd stood there and blatantly said she wouldn't mind having a man like me."

"I remember," Raylene's neck rolled. "I also remember that *you stayed.* Why didn't you say something to her? As the pastor, I would think it wouldn't be a problem to let a woman know that her advances are not acceptable, especially to the pastor of the church."

"I'm a man, Ray."

She curled her lips in disgust. "Great, now you're just a man. What next, you'll deny being an adult?"

"Preachers have to be careful when dealing with women like Felicia. They're dangerous and can ruin an entire career. What was I supposed to say to her without offending her and causing a scandal?"

"How about 'Stop?' How about 'No? Get off me? I'm engaged!'" She could go on, but it was only adding up to wasting her breath.

Her condemnation must have pissed him off, because Will got up and headed for the front door. "My actions to reconcile were obviously a mistake."

Raylene followed him out, yelling at him all the way to the car. "You got that right! You get a quickie from that wench and have the gall to even fix your pathetic mouth to accuse me of having something to do with it. Yeah, Will, you coming over here was a mistake!"

He was halfway down the sidewalk when he turned and

looked at her. The expression on his face was lost. "Baby, I still love you," he said. "Take your time and pray about it. I believe God will see us through and you will be Mrs. Willard Vernal Robinson on the day we've planned to marry." Then in a last attempt at hitting her where it counted, Will said, "Raylene, what would Jesus do?"

"He'd make you go home!" She belted back. "So go home, Will! Go home!" Then, in a move of second-hand haste, Raylene looked toward the sky with a pitiful look of appeal. "Lord, forgive me."

Raylene turned and went inside without waiting for Will to drive off. She closed the door behind her and went to her room. She really had no idea what Jesus would do . . . because she wasn't Jesus.

THELMA HEARD THE FRONT DOOR OPEN and close. She peeked down the hall only to catch Raylene storming down it before disappearing into her room.

"Who was that?"

"Jehovah's Witness."

Raylene stepped inside her room and closed the door, obviously not wanting to talk about the encounter.

Thelma let it slide. She knew Raylene wasn't telling the truth. She'd looked out the window and seen Will's car parked in front of the house. She also heard Raylene hollering at him. But she wasn't going to make an issue of it. Raylene needed this wake-up call.

Thelma ducked back inside her room and finished getting ready. She still hadn't decided what shoes she was going to wear. She'd been to the Gypsy Tea Room before and was familiar with the standing-only policy, so she was trying to decide on a pair of designer loafers or the brand-new pair of Nikes that were still in the box. She'd opted for jeans and a pullover for comfort, nothing dressy. She'd long ago abandoned the idea of getting all churched up for concerts.

Monroe was posted up on her bed like a fat rat in an empty cheese truck.

She shook her head at the dog. "I told you not to eat that beef loaf all at once." Thelma sat on the bed and elected the Nikes as she fussed. "Maybe next time you'll listen to me."

She got up and double-checked herself in the mirror once she was fully dressed. She looked good, all 160 pounds of her. At five seven, this made her an admirable thick-but-fine. She grabbed her earrings and slid the hooks into her ear holes, frosted her lips with a salmon shade of pink, and dabbed scented oil behind her ears and in her cleavage.

"And don't lie up in here and fart in my bed, either. I don't want to come back to a room smelling like the walls are made of dog ass, you got it?"

Monroe wagged his tail, whined, and rolled over on his side. "Don't beg." She shot the dog a sympathetic stare. "You know I don't like it when you beg. As a matter of fact, I don't want you in my room while I'm gone tonight."

Monroe got up and carefully leaped from the bed. He poked his nose into the door's crack and eased his body through.

"Male dogs," Thelma groaned. "They aren't any better sometimes." She talked to no one in particular as she posed one last time in the mirror, checking both sides of her booty from the back. Tight and good. She turned, brushed down her front, and checked the details. She needed a fill and retouch on her nails and hair, but even those didn't take away from how well the outfit put a smooth finish on her full hips and C-cup breasts.

She turned on the stereo in her room and tucked a towel on the floor, into the space at the bottom of the door. Janis Joplin blared through the speakers as Thelma kneeled down and reached under the bed. She pulled out a wooden cigar box, placed the box on the bed, and opened it. She was familiar with everything inside: incense, a dime bag half full, a roller, a pocketknife, and two blunt wraps, honey flavored. It was time for her to cool out, like she only did every so often after an energy-devouring day at the hospital.

Thelma lit an incense, cut the wrap, emptied the tobacco, crumbled the grass, and rolled a fresh blunt with the roller. She'd told Raylene she'd be ready by seven thirty, which gave her thirty minutes to make good on her word. While she smoked, Thelma cased the bookshelf in her room. It relaxed her. As she studied the titles, her eyes landed on *From the Palm of My Hand*, Marcus Brooks's first book and the only one she liked. She leafed through the pages and wondered if the author was ever going to write a book as great as his first. Had she not had to perform surgery on a German shepherd, she would have been at the station, waiting for the opportunity to ask.

She puffed on the blunt and thumped its ashes into a nearby homemade ashtray. Thelma turned off Janis. She reached for the guitar near her bed, where she sat, and cradled it on her knee. It was a Palmer acoustic, her first guitar, a gift she'd given to herself when she turned sixteen, over nineteen years ago. The guitar rested against an Emerson amplifier that served as both speaker and nightstand. Thelma plugged the guitar in, checked the tuning, and began to play a song she'd written.

You're a liar
and a lonely man
I trusted you
gave you my hand
but you never could unlock your mind
Where's the key?
And now you wanna enforce your shit on me
making my friends strangers
Expecting me to believe
Now all I have is anger
I had a name
long 'fore you came
and I'll be damned
if I get strange.
Just 'cause you think your reason is tighter than my rhyme.
The wine is sweeter only the first time.
The wine is sweeter only the first time.

It was soul music. She hoped to someday sell some of her songs, but for now, they lay hidden away in her notebooks.

She heard her door open. She looked up and saw Raylene peeking in.

"Thelma Linell Wade." Raylene was shocked. "Girl, I cannot believe you smoke reefer. You ought to be ashamed of yourself."

"You ought to be ashamed for still calling it reefer." Thelma giggled. "You never really know someone until you live with them."

"Whatever. Weed, then. I'm still shocked."

"Aw, damn, Raylene. Don't act like you have never needed to do the unthinkable just to keep the weight of the world off your shoulders. Nobody's perfect."

"I say nope to dope."

"No wonder you're so illiberal and stuffy."

Raylene waved the smoke away. "That stuff serves no purpose." She gagged. "And it stinks."

"Speak for yourself." Thelma laughed and got off the subject. "So, how are you feeling?"

"My preacher boyfriend fiancé cheated on me—how do you think I feel?"

"Probably like you've swallowed the ocean instead of a simple glass of water. Or maybe I'm wrong and you actually feel guilt."

"Don't you start in on me too," she broke in. "It's bad enough Gwena and Naomi think I'm partially at fault. Don't tell me you side with them and Will too."

"No. I'm not siding with Will. I'll never side with a man who lets his Johnson think for him, but I will never side with a woman who doesn't get down for hers when it's time to show her man that she's serious about being with him, including pastors. I won't protect you from facing the truth."

"Will asked *me* to marry him, so why am I being convicted for his infidelity."

"You said yes, didn't you?"

"Yeah, but I shouldn't have to beat women down to keep him."

"What I'm trying to say is that I told you Felicia Henderson was after Will a long time ago, and what did you do about it?"

"Why should I have to do anything?"

"Because you set the standards for how you want to live and be treated and perceived. If not for Will, then for Raylene."

"Look, can we drop the subject please?" Raylene sighed. "Will's actions got us here, not my lack of reaction." She sank onto the bed.

"Suit yourself." Thelma put the blunt out, returned what was left to the box, and slid it back under the bed. Then, she began strumming a different tune.

Raylene rocked to the song. "Is that new?"

"Yeah. You like it?"

"I do. It reminds me of being on a mountain overlooking the earth."

Thelma laughed. "Thanks. I'm thinking of publishing a catalog. Who knows? Maybe I'll someday be on stage accepting a Grammy."

"You have what it takes." Raylene's voice broke. "Your songs have always been an inspiration to me."

"Would you miss me if I moved to New York or L.A.?"

"Of course I would."

"It'd be me and Monroe leveling out the dirt on the road less traveled."

Raylene cut her eyes at Thelma. "You need to find you a man and stop carrying that dog everywhere with you."

"What I need a man for?" Thelma laughed. "Men are only good for three things that I call the three S's: sex, socializing, and seeing about my tires."

Thelma was serious, but Raylene reeled over laughing anyway.

"I'm not kidding. Men like to keep it simple, and women should do the same. We give those fools too much credit, and for what? Buying a wedding ring and a big house? Shit, I can do that for myself."

Raylene got up and held her hand up in the air. "Sweetie,

you're high, and I'm in no mood for a sermon, speech, lecture, or commentary on how much you can do without a man, especially when I'm having trouble with mine. You shouldn't smoke, Thelma. It will kill you."

"So will lightning and guns." Thelma had learned all her smoker's comeback lines. She glanced at the time. "We have to go. I've got to know what happened with Marcus Brooks on the *Lamont Troy Show* today. Gwena said all hell broke loose in the studio."

Raylene picked up the book, turning it over to the full-scale black-and-white photo of Marcus, and studied it.

"Where'd he get this nose?"

Thelma leaned over and looked. "He didn't buy it—that's for sure. His honker is home grown."

"You don't think he's attractive?"

"He's all right, but he ain't nothing to have an orgasm over.

"I heard he assaulted one of the staff," Raylene said. "Will told me the police were looking for him."

"That's a shame," Thelma said, sounding disappointed. "He is a primary example of why I say niggas ain't shit and should be put to sleep. Men like Marcus Brooks serve this world no good."

"I thought you liked him?"

"No, I liked his first book. There's a difference. I've never cut for him as a person. I think Marcus Brooks is an opinionated big mouth who has too much time on his hands, so he uses it to put all his pitiful little thoughts on paper, package them up, and sell it to the public."

"Have you ever met him?"

"No," Thelma admitted. "I'd be in jail or dead by now if that were the case, because I'm sure we would not get along. I don't care how attractive he is, you hear me?" She turned off the lights.

"He's good looking, I will say that much," Raylene agreed. "If he weren't such an ass, would you date him?"

"I don't date."

"Then what do you do?"

"I told you, I get what I need and I move on."

"Thelma, that ain't right."

"Neither is getting caught in the choir closet with a sinner. I don't date, because men aren't into that so why should I be?"

"Because you deserve love and to be loved."

"I love me. I love me all the time."

"You think Marcus has ever had love in his life?"

"Men like Marcus reject love like crack babies reject human touch. Marcus's problem is that he doesn't know when to shut up, so he can never receive. He's so busy preaching his point of view. He has no room for love."

Raylene's curiosity piqued. "How do you know?"

"It's in his writing. It's in his interviews. It's in the editorials and the short stories he writes. I used to be a big fan until he started calling women bitches as if the public really needed to hear him say that all the time. I'm familiar with his work enough to know. He likes being a shock magnet."

"A what?" Raylene giggled. She was probably getting a contact high.

"He shocks people into buying his books. But me? I beat a nigga down for calling me a bitch or calling another woman a bitch in front of me." Thelma tapped her own butt in an openly conceited fashion. "You can't let 'em get away with it; otherwise, we're a part of the problem."

"What do you know?" Raylene smiled teasingly. "You could meet him and experience love at first sight."

"Honey, please." Thelma waved off the comment. "A brother has to be pretty special to make me think about allowing my eyes to dictate how I feel about him." She looked at her watch. "Time to go."

"I'm driving." Raylene giggled. "You're under the influence."

Thelma didn't argue. Raylene was her optimistic, good-hearted, romantic friend who had seemed to be down for whatever, but feared breaking the law, otherwise.

She put her guitar back in the case, tidied up, and grabbed her purse. As she closed the door, the idea of being in love crossed her mind again. "Love . . . no way," she said before locking the door behind her.

MARCUS SNEAKED OUT of his hotel room at the Adolphus and took the service door exit. He footed it out of downtown and checked into the Linny Inn on the outskirts. It was a single-level motel with no more than thirty units surrounding a nearly vacant parking lot. The man who checked him in didn't even ask for an ID or credit card. The police would never find him here.

His room was small and smelled of smoke. The television was missing knobs, and the carpet was stained with what looked like hot iron scorches and coffee. The bed was made, but the bed-spread was faded and ripped on one of the corners. The entire surrounding was depressing.

He used his cell phone to call Regis. When he heard the agent's voice, Marcus felt saved. Regis would be able to make the necessary calls to get Marcus the professional legal assistance he required.

"Regis, this is Marcus. I need your help."

"So the chicken has finally come home to roost with the Jew," Regis replied in a flat tone. "A cold day in hell, is it?"

Marcus didn't have time to play. This was serious. "Regis, this bitch down here has filed assault charges against me, and I need you to call me a lawyer. The police are looking for me."

"You fired me, remember?"

Marcus gritted his teeth. "Then I'm hiring you back."

"Are you still in Dallas?" Regis asked.

The author let out an impatient sigh. "Yes, and I need legal counsel before the authorities catch up with me."

"I think I'm going to let you sit this one out, Mr. Brooks. Call me when you get back to Atlanta. Have a nice time in Dallas . . . jailbird."

Marcus looked at his phone. "You, matzo-ball-eating bastard! Just for that, consider your pink slip in the mail!" he yelled, and in a fit of anger, Marcus tossed the cell phone across the room, shattering it into pieces. He sat on the bed until nightfall, wondering how in the hell he was going to get out of his situation. He was a wanted man.

It was nearing eleven, and he'd grown restless in the small room with no air-conditioning. Several of the units around him that were being reserved had opened doors and windows. He could even hear a couple getting it on two doors down.

He decided to take a walk to a nearby bar and get a drink. There was action down the way, and that's what the author needed, some action.

Marcus grabbed his satchel and draped it across his chest before sliding the room key into his pocket.

The Dallas streets were a far cry from Atlanta, which had areas like this one but full of black folk. He missed home. He missed waking up in his own bed. He missed looking out his window overlooking a pleasant courtyard. He missed Piedmont Park, the Underground, his freedom. Marcus missed being a free and unwanted man.

As he walked down the street and crossed Main into a dark parking lot, he saw the shadow of a vagrant woman running up to him. She was a beggar. Marcus gripped his satchel strap in case she had some of her homeless homies waiting in the shadows to mug him. He hated the homeless. He hated how lazy they were and how effortless it was to just be around and not take on any responsibilities. Especially the crackheads and cardboard-box-holding peddlers that invaded intersection corners and sidewalks with signs that read shit like WILL WORK FOR FOOD.

His mother would say that if a man was strong enough to hold up a sign, then he was strong enough to pick up a pen and fill out a job application. But Junesta just talked big because no matter what she said about vagrants and the unfortunate, she always found two dollars to freely give the very person she'd just insulted. "Jesus loves a cheerful giver," she'd say to her son. "So always give."

And in that moment, Marcus was willing to give. Maybe God would bless his cheerful giving and in the morning this entire event would be a bad dream. There would be no charges against him. There would be no evidence of shoes thrown. There would be no sneaking out of a five-star hotel to stay in a starless motel, and this entire trip to Dallas would be to his advantage.

JONNIE COLEMAN CASED THE STREETS of Deep Ellum looking for a stranger with a giving face. She wasn't in the mood for any mess tonight. She'd had a rough day and needed a pack of smokes and some beer, which she was about seven dollars away from having. Tonight, she would have to put her best skills forward, even if she had to do a little knee work. She didn't consider herself a prostitute or a beggar, even though she qualified high in both categories. A homeless crackhead she was not. Jonnie Coleman was just poor in all the wrong places.

The heated summer nights had the Dallas streets slowly crawling with the regulars and a few weekenders who were club-hopping, drinking, or both. As she walked down Main Street away from the core of the activity, Jonnie thought about where she would start panhandling. Unfortunately, the crowded areas were already being worked by other panhandlers, many of them folks she knew. She'd already passed by several of them, all attempting to collect enough money for their vices. Jonnie's friends had names such as Homeless Ricky, Geneva With The Seven Kids, K-K, Newt, Philly Phil (from Harlem by way of Chi-Town), and Bean.

Jonnie crossed Main and walked past the Gypsy Tea Room. It was a moderate double-sided-size club where she could get a little action when it was packed, and tonight it was jumping. She could tell from standing in the door and peeking in each time it was opened—the place was filled, and a live band was playing. She recognized the song and began dancing on the sidewalk in front of the doorway.

It was an old but popular George Benson tune. Jonnie shook her hips and snapped her fingers with her hands in the air like a belly dancer. "Hey, that's my song!" She stepped lively and sang along. "I won't quit till I'm a star, on Broadway."

"All right, Jonnie. That's enough. Get away from the door. You're blocking business." A man's voice came from the club entrance.

Jonnie stopped dancing and looked at Rufus, the security guy who knew her face. He worked the door whenever a big event was happening.

"Rufus, lemme bum a smoke off you, man," she asked.

He pointed to her neck. "What happened to you?"

"Dog bite," Jonnie said holding up her hand. "Don't ask—just give me a cigarette."

The muscular security guy raised the sleeve of his T-shirt, revealing an odd-looking bandage. "I quit. I'm on the patch."

Jonnie swatted him off. "That stuff don't work. All it's gon' do is give you the shits."

Rufus laughed. "Yeah, but my breath won't stink anymore, and my lungs will thank me for it. You should try it sometime."

"When yo' lungs learn to talk, I want you to call me so I can put you in a freak show," she said. "Until then, I need to come upon some change to get me some smokes."

"I'm wiped out tonight. Sorry."

Jonnie understood, because when the young doorman had money, he'd always give her a nice donation. And on special occasions, he'd chip in and get her a twelve-pack and a carton of Newports.

Suddenly, another man—who was smaller than Rufus and had squared shoulders, a drink in his hand, and a fancy suit—came barging through the door. He was bowl-faced, no older than thirty, with slick hair and bloodshot eyes.

It was Cecil, the manager. He walked up to Jonnie and pushed her back, shining his flashlight on her. "No loitering! I've told you people to stop hanging around my club. Don't make me call the police."

Jonnie leaned back. "Get that light off me, man!" she shouted while shielding her eyes. She wasn't backing down. "You young punk-ass boy think you hot pastrami 'cause you manage some shit? Well, I'm telling you it ain't shit!"

Jonnie spat on the sidewalk near the man's feet and bolted off toward the dark parking lot half a block up.

The streetlight had been knocked out, but Jonnie was more comfortable in the darkness anyway. She knew the night streets better than the day streets.

As she walked, she could hear the laughter and cackles of a group of women behind her. Jonnie turned and cased them as she walked backwards to check them out as possible givers.

There were five of them: a tall one, a short one, a fat one, and two that were about midsize, except one of them had hips, and she had the outfit on to prove it. They were an attractive bunch, well dressed, cleanly groomed, and they all looked like they had money. Jonnie wondered who had the most giving face, because that would be who she approached first. The tall one was singing the George Benson tune. Jonnie decided not to ask her because she was tall and she liked to look her potential givers in the eye when she asked them for money. Besides, the woman was talking loud, which meant she was probably drunk, and Jonnie resisted peddling to drunk folk. They usually had the guts to say no.

She decided to avoid the drunk one of the group and approach the petite one with the ponytail weave instead. They stood about the same height, build, and size, even though Jonnie's own hips and breasts were now victims of time and gravity, and her hair was cornrowed under a dingy Dallas Mavericks' baseball cap.

Jonnie had to admit, even wigs and weaves had evolved from when she was growing up. Now, it was hard to tell real hair from the fake.

Besides, the petite woman had on designer everything, and her weave was laid tighter than any real hairstyle Jonnie had ever seen. She was bound to be the one of the group to come off money.

The women were leaving the Gypsy, which meant they were probably carrying lots of random dollar bills that had not been used to tip the bartender.

Jonnie rubbed her hands together. "A'ight, here we go," she said to herself.

Not wanting to be noticed, she ran ahead, staying out of view. As she crossed the first aisle, she put herself right in the path of a young man who had the face of a nonlocal. When she bumped into him, he pushed her away.

"Sorry, brother," she said. Then her night vision allowed her to get a good look at the stranger. He was fine, handsomely dressed, and alone. Jonnie immediately began to put her mack down. "Hey, now," Jonnie sang as she perked her breasts out and put her hands on her hips. "You need a little extra something something? I can gift you for twenty bucks."

The man backed up. "Excuse me?"

"Okay, five." Jonnie knew how to bargain.

Still no response.

"I'm talking about a blow job, honey." Jonnie cleared her throat. How about I take you around the corner and hook you up?"

The man shifted his weight and adjusted the satchel that hung from his shoulder. "Are you out of your mind?"

Jonnie let his remark slide. She changed her angle and hit him up for cash instead of ass. "Oh, my bad, brother," she apologized. "But can you spare a sister a dime? Anything you got to give will be appreciated. I'm just tryin' to get a pack of smokes and some beer for the night." Telling the truth worked well for her. She stuttered when she lied, and Jonnie didn't like to stutter, so she lied only when she had to.

The man hesitated and huffed like a spoiled child as he reached for his wallet. "You crackhead hos make me sick, always begging." His face grew stoic as he took two dollars from his pocket and held them out to Jonnie as if she had muddy hands and he were in a white suit. "Here."

She bridled at the comment. Jonnie didn't appreciate being called something she definitely was not. She considered it an insult. She had a home, she didn't steal for drugs, and she wasn't jittery like those stalemates over off of Ervay, which to many was crackhead row. Jonnie wasn't going to let it slide. "I ain't no damned crackhead," she blasted. "I may be a ho sometimes, but I ain't no crackhead, ever! Your mama's the crackhead." Jonnie snatched the dollars from his hand and stepped back. "Now you have a nice night, fella."

She moseyed away until she felt hands grab her and toss her to the ground. She peered about wild-eyed, suddenly struck with confusion and horror until she felt the stranger pummel her with slaps and grabs.

"Give me my money back!" The stranger ordered as he wrapped his arms around Jonnie's, locking in a firm grip over the hand that was holding the two bucks. He wrapped his fingers around her fist, squeezing her bones into one another, and began prying her bony fingers apart from the cash.

Jonnie did all she could to protect the income. "Let me go!" She strained as she tightened her clutch on the bills.

His grip made her knuckles feel like they were being crushed. She yowled out in pain, but she stayed resistant.

Jonnie worked like a dog to hold on to the money, but found it about to be a losing battle. Her hand stung, and she wondered if any of her fingers had been broken. She was barely one hundred pounds, and this man had to be at least 170, 180. He could crush her whole body if he wanted to. With the right amount of force and fortitude, the stranger would have his money back in no time and Jonnie would be back at square one, which she wasn't in favor of, so she did the next best thing. With the strongest breath she could muster, Jonnie Coleman began to yell for help.

MARCUS DIDN'T CARE who saw him contesting the old woman with the Band-Aid on her neck. He wanted his money back, because nobody but nobody insulted his mother. He'd be damned before he was going to let some crackhead in denial say anything about the woman who brought him into this world and get away with it—plus two of his hard-earned dollars.

The vagrant's body odor burned his nostrils, but the smell of rhinoceros ass in the summer couldn't keep him from taking back what was his in the first place. Marcus started shaking her. If he couldn't take the money, he'd shake the shit out of her and maybe she'd drop it.

"Hey! Leave that woman alone!" A female voice came from the darkness. It was followed by a sister in a dress, and the click of her heels rushed toward him.

"Stay out of this," he ordered. Marcus pushed the old woman to the ground with such force, she went reeling into the bumper of a nearby SUV, where she landed and howled out in pain. Then he stood over her, grabbed the neck of her shirt, and prepared to hit her some more.

Now Marcus noticed the woman calling out to him was four friends deep and about seventy pounds overburdened. They were all faceless shadows to him, nothing to worry about.

Sweat beads now glistened on his face, but he wasn't concerned. All he wanted was his two dollars, and he wasn't about to let some good citizen stand in his way.

He eyed the silhouettes of the small group of approaching women. If he weren't trying to get to the old lady, he'd definitely be putting his mack down, especially to the one in the fitted jeans and white sneakers that seemed to glow beneath the shadows.

"You ladies need to mind your business." He shifted the satchel on his shoulder. "This crackhead is trying to steal two dollars from me," he informed them.

"You slimy mud duck!" The old woman continued to fight against his hold on her. "I done told you once I ain't no crackhead, and you gave me this money!" She shook her balled fist at him. The bills remained stiff in her grip. "It was a donation."

"That doesn't give you reason to put your hands on her." The woman he was admiring just seconds ago was now close enough for him to see. She was exactly his height and looked like she worked out, but Marcus didn't cower. He tossed the old woman to the side. She fell to the ground between him and the women with a loud grunt of air being knocked from her.

"Let her go. She could use the money more than you, Mr. Designer Outfit and Leather Bag." She had a mouth on her too, he noticed.

Marcus stood his ground. "Look, lady. I asked you once to mind your own goddamned business! When I get my money, then I'll be on my way." He returned his attention to getting his cash. At the same time, three of the women all walked his way as well. Night felt like high noon, and the old woman must have felt like ice at a hell festival.

The woman with the hat on backed away from Marcus, and rightfully so, as she seemed to be the only one intimidated by his anger. The women made it to the beggar first and surrounded her, creating a barricade.

The heavyset one of the group went into her purse and stepped to him. She was wearing a black dress, but the slimming effect didn't work. If he had to call it, she needed to be somewhere romancing a treadmill. She pulled out some cash. "Here's five dollars. Take it and leave her alone."

"I don't want *your* money." Marcus shook his head and pointed at the vagrant. "That's *my* money she's holding right there. It came out of my wallet. Move out of the way and turn that smart-mouthed bitch over to me."

"Wait a minute," the tall one thundered. "That was uncalled for." She separated from the others and resolutely charged up to him. "We don't play that around here."

The liquor on her breath burned his nostrils. Whatever she drank, it was strong.

He stood his ground. "The last time I checked, this was a free country," he replied. "And you need to get out of my face."

The woman who had offered the money held the five-dollar bill out again. "Look, mister. Just take the money. We don't want to start any trouble."

"Too late," he said. "You've already started it."

"You're Marcus Brooks," the youngest-looking of the group said.

"That's right, and I'm a man who is simply trying to take back what is mine."

The woman tucked the money back into her purse and grabbed her friend's arm. "Thelma, let's go. He's not worth it."

"So, Sasquatch has a name? Now I have something to tell the Dallas police when this is all over." Marcus smirked.

Thelma jerked from the grip of her friend in the black dress. "We're not leaving this woman for him to beat up, and I think the police would be happy to see you walk into the station. We know they're looking for you."

The situation had turned.

The old woman stepped up next to Thelma. "I ain't giving up shit! I worked hard for this two dollars, he gave it to me, and it's mines!"

"Don't I know you?" Thelma asked.

"No." The old woman tried to avoid Thelma's eyes.

"Yes, I do," Thelma said. "Jonnie Coleman, right? You came to my hospital this morning." Thelma nodded and gave the woman a sympathetic look. "Don't worry—you can keep your money."

The woman in the black dress raised her voice. "Let's go."

Marcus warned, "Thelma, you better listen to fatso before this gets ugly."

The heavyset woman didn't take offense. Instead she made another attempt at getting Thelma to back down. "Thelma, let's go." This time her voice begged.

"We're not going anywhere until this *nigga* apologizes for the name-calling and goes on about his business." She pushed her friend farther away. She was stronger than she looked and for the first time doubt entered Marcus's head.

She must have been the leader of the pack because the fat one stepped back and waited to see what was going to happen.

"Ladies, don't be afraid of her because she's drunk," he said, trying to skillfully maneuver out of the dubious situation without looking like a coward. "Go ahead and tell her how embarrassing she is all drunk and hot in the mouth." He looked at Thelma. "You are embarrassing your friends, don't you think?"

"Girl, kick his ass!" The youngest-looking woman dressed in the tight skirt and shoulder-revealing top hollered out.

"I don't need you instigating," he said. "As a matter of fact, one more word from any of you tramps, and this shit *is* going to get physical. All I want is my money."

Thelma balled her fists. "We've already told you to go on about your business. We won't say it again."

"I'm not scared of you, Amazon." Marcus bragged. "Tricks like you are no match for a man like me."

The woman in the sneakers lunged at him with such quickness, he didn't know what hit him. Suddenly he was in a headlock. Marcus thought his head was going to explode.

"Are you going to apologize?"

"Hell no!" He winced. Marcus slapped and clawed at her grip, but to no avail. He was caught.

Thelma flexed her toned arm around his head, tightening her death clutch. "It's men like you that make women like me sick to my stomach. You got three seconds to apologize or else I'm going to snap your neck." She maintained her grip on him. "One . . ."

Marcus felt the heat rising in his face, but he wasn't going to back down for a bunch of well-dressed female thugs from Dallas. He debated giving up, but that would mean he wasn't the man he thought himself to be; then he thought about dying.

"Two . . ."

He thought about the trouble he was already in and realized he really had nothing to live for anyway.

"Three."

"Fuck you," Marcus managed to say, not caring that they were potentially his last words. His vision blurred as he struggled in her hold.

And like that, the grip became so constricting, spittle oozed from his lips, and Marcus began to lose consciousness.

THELMA WASN'T INTERESTED in letting Marcus Brooks live. He was nothing short of a nuisance, one the world really didn't need. Any man that could find it in himself to beat on and curse women should be put to sleep, just like a dog. At least that's the way she saw it. Besides, this one in particular had refused to make amends with a simple apology, so it was time to shut him down and pay the consequences later.

"Thelma, don't kill him!" Naomi cried out. "He's not worth it." She ran over to Thelma and began pulling on her arms.

Thelma had lost it somewhere inside her own angry thoughts. She released her hold on him.

Marcus fell to the ground, coughing and gasping for breath.

"We need to go before he gets up," Gwena said.

Thelma noticed her standing away from everyone else. "What are you doing way over there?"

"Staying out of this mess, and if you all were smart, you'd listen to me and come on."

Thelma asked Jonnie, "Can we take you anywhere and drop you off?"

"No, I'm pretty much home already. I don't live far from here." She stuffed the money past her pants, down into her underwear. "But can I have that five?"

Latice handed over the bill. "Here."

Thelma saw Marcus get back on his feet. His motions were

clumsy and wobbled. He stood watching them, his breathing so intense, his chest moved in and out in the shadows.

Thelma prepared herself for another round as he charged at her again.

"It's on now," he said, his own pose resembling that of the Karate Kid. He swung at her, but Thelma quickly moved out of his reach.

She was ready. He was underestimating her, and that pissed her off even more. She was a trained boxer and a brown belt in karate. She'd studied everyone from Bruce Lee to Lennox Lewis and was certified in kicking ass.

When her left hook connected with his nose, blood skeeted out and stained her top. Marcus wailed out in pain, and his knees buckled, but he didn't let that stop him. Instead, he came back for more.

His technique wasn't much of a technique at all. He looked like a clown trying to fight. Marcus moved slow and would be easy to knock out. She sized him up as she studied his build and movements, never taking her eyes from his balled fists. Marcus wasn't as tall as she was or as massive, but he was muscular, and that stood for something in the fighting world. Thelma would have to be careful. He tried a roundhouse punch but once again found himself vulnerable.

She blocked her face with one fist and landed a right hook to his jaw with the other, sending him tumbling back to the ground. Her knuckles stung. They would be bruised tomorrow. "Now I don't need an apology. I kicked your ass."

"Oooh, shit. That's the best matchup I've seen in a long time," Jonnie hooted. "Honey, you fight like that Ali girl."

Marcus rolled around on the ground, his body locked into a fetal position as he made an effort to cradle his pain.

"Now we can go," she said, turning her back on him. She dusted herself off as best she could, but her outfit had been soiled.

Suddenly Thelma felt herself being rushed from behind and

into the side of one of the parked automobiles. Fire spread through the pit of her stomach, her ribs, and her knees as they connected with the car. The wind had been knocked from her.

She heard Naomi and Raylene gasp as Marcus stepped back and waited for her to turn around. When she did, he right-handed her to her midsection and knocked the air from her again. She fell over, cringing.

Marcus fought dirty, something Thelma didn't believe in, nor was she prepared for it. He pulled her away from the car and slapped her. The skin on her face burned, and her neck ached. She concentrated on breathing and keeping her eyes on him. As long as she was aware, she knew she could regain control. She felt her left eye swell to a closed slit.

Thelma bounced back quickly. She found a comfortable defensive stance and waited.

When she felt the right moment come along, Thelma found an open shot and took it, landing another left to his eye. It was Hammer Time in Thelmaville.

"Thelma, no more!" Raylene yelled as she ran over and tried to get Thelma to back down. She was only pushed to the side.

"Raylene, get back," Thelma warned. "He obviously doesn't know when enough is enough."

"Yeah, bitch." Marcus spat out blood. "I know when enough is enough." He rushed her again.

The two locked in a violent tug and began struggling against each other. They wavered together for several feet, each clawing and throwing punches. Thelma would land a punch and then have one landed on her. Blood oozed from her lips, and she could taste the salty bitterness as she licked the cut. Marcus drove his body into hers, and she attempted to push back, but her feet got crossed, making her shoe come off. Thelma lost her footing and tumbled backwards. Marcus took the opportunity to force her to the ground, climb on top of her, and wrap his hands around her neck.

Raylene screamed.

Thelma wiggled beneath his weight as she felt her oxygen grow short. She scratched the back of his hands, but the grip around her neck was fixed, and he was determined to put an end to the fight. Her air passages felt like they were being superglued shut.

Gwena took off toward the cars. "I'm calling the police."

"Hurry!" Naomi said as she tried to pull Marcus off Thelma without any luck. Marcus was strong, and Thelma already knew that she'd lost her chance at shutting him down by being careless with her footwork.

Her feet slowly lost their kick as she gasped spastically for breath. Marcus pulled her head up by the neck and began pounding it against the concrete. Thelma felt herself losing consciousness, and for the first time that night, the thought of death crossed her mind. The last thing she heard was Raylene's chilling scream. Hammer Time in Thelmaville was coming to an end.

GWENA SPRINTED TO THE CAR. She felt like God was playing a cruel joke on her, and the punch line was Marcus.

As she frantically unlocked the door, Gwena tried to talk herself through it without losing her cool. It was a coping mechanism she'd learned in therapy. It kept the anxiety from attacking.

"Gwena," she said. "Now is not the time to panic." Then, in cheesy horror-movie fashion, she dropped the keys and they fell out of sight. Gwena could hear the scuffle still happening in the distance as she blindly felt for the keys in the darkness. After what seemed like forever, she finally found them. This time she held the keys securely in her hands, opened the car door, and grabbed her phone.

The car was stuffy, more suffocating than the air had become, so she stepped back into the night to make the call. As she dialed the emergency number, a scream came through the air so gut-shattering, Gwena startled and dropped the phone. It crashed into pieces against the concrete.

It was Raylene's voice, and her wail was nothing short of terrifying. Gwena ran to the lane to see what was going on.

There in the shadows underneath Marcus was Thelma, still and lifeless.

Raylene, Naomi, and Latice were pulling on him, but to no avail; he was stronger than all three of them.

Instinctively, Gwena grabbed a five-pound dumbbell and

flashlight from the exercise bag she kept in the car and raced back as fast as her legs would carry her. She rushed up behind Marcus, who was now banging Thelma's head against the concrete. If it were up to her, Thelma wasn't going to die, but Marcus might.

She raised the weight like Tiger Woods going in for the Masters victory, and with one powerful swing she whacked Marcus across the side of his head with all the strength she had in her. The dull-sounding thud of the weight against his skull sent chills through her, starting at her hand and flowing down through the pit of her stomach and back up to her head, making her dizzy. Gwena felt sick.

Marcus grabbed his head. He turned to catch a glimpse of his attacker. She saw him focus through his pain, and attempt an effortless reach for her.

Gwena stepped away and flashed the light in his eyes, blinding him.

Marcus reeled away from the bright glare.

Then, in a last act of defense, Gwena lifted the dumbbell again and swung at him, this time knocking him out cold.

Marcus fell to the concrete as a small trickle of blood made its way down the side of his head.

Gwena dropped the weight and observed the damage.

She saw Raylene run to the side of a car and throw up.

Gwena felt bad for going to such an extreme, but she was the only one who understood that when it came to Marcus Brooks, they were in a kill-or-possibly-be-killed situation.

LATICE WAS THE FIRST to move toward where Marcus lay bleeding and unconscious. The blood trickling from his head put a knot in her stomach unlike any she'd ever felt before. She leaned down and checked for a pulse. "He's still alive," she reported. "Thank the good Lord."

Naomi eased over to get a closer look. "Gwena, did you have to hit him that hard?" she asked. "Wasn't once enough?"

"Naomi, he could have killed Thelma."

"How do you know?"

"Look at her! She looks like she ran into Mike Tyson's fist!"

Thelma shifted on the concrete. "I'm okay. I look worse than I feel."

Latice held up her hand. "That's good to hear." She looked around for Raylene. "Are you okay?"

"Well . . . considering I almost witnessed a murder," Raylene replied. "I'm not too well." She wiped spittle from her mouth with the sleeve of her shirt.

"One thing's for sure," Thelma said from the ground where she still sat. "He won't be hitting any more women tonight."

Gwena huffed. "But he's going to be a monster when he wakes up. We should get going."

Jonnie Coleman inched over, grabbed Marcus's wallet, snatched the cash from it, and dashed off, toward traffic.

"Hey! Come back here!" Latice yelled out.

Jonnie's dark thin legs moved a lot quicker than anyone would expect. None of them would be able to catch her except Thelma. However, Thelma was in no condition for running. Blood stained both knees on her pant legs.

Jonnie made it to the other side of a semi-busy street before she turned around and looked their way. "I only come back for money, honey!" Then Jonnie turned around and zipped off into the darkness.

"Ain't that a bitch?" Gwena said. "The least she could have done was thanked us for saving her ass."

Thelma touched her eye, which was now quite swollen. "Ow."

"We have bigger fish to fry," Naomi said. "Gwena, were you able to call the police?"

Gwena shook her head. "I dropped my phone. Broke it."

Raylene hurriedly fished her phone from her purse. "I have mine." Then, she offered the phone out. "Someone else will have to make the call. I wouldn't know what to say." Her voice shook.

"You tell them what happened and tell them to hurry because Marcus Brooks is injured," Gwena replied. "You tell them the truth."

In that moment it hit her. Latice had an epiphany. "Wait," she said. "I have an idea."

"Uh-oh," Naomi said. "The last time you had an idea, we all ended up doing the dishes at Denny's."

"It wasn't my idea that had us washing dishes," Latice said. "It was Raylene's ass."

"Playing Eat and Run was your idea." Raylene took offense. "Don't blame me because I left Will's birthday present behind and had to go back and get it. What were you expecting me to do?" Then Raylene pointed at Gwena. "You were the one who turned herself in first anyway, so what are you talking about?"

"That gift didn't even have his name on it," Latice said at Raylene. "You could have left it."

Gwena began shaking her head in defense. "Right is right, and wrong is wrong. We shouldn't have tried to eat and run in the first place."

"Excuse us," Thelma interrupted. "If we don't do something soon, we won't have a choice but to call the police."

Gwena's eyes scouted the darkness as she talked to Latice. "What are you thinking?"

Latice looked at the women. "Ladies, I know you're going to think I'm crazy, but what if we took him home and cleaned him up? Maybe then he wouldn't press charges. We could convince him with kindness."

"You're right," Gwena said. "I think you're crazy." She moved around away from Latice. "No. I think you're insane."

"We need to get him to a hospital," Naomi said. "He could have a concussion."

"Let him lay there," Thelma said. "Fuck him.ľ"

"Thelma, we can't just leave him here."

"Why not, Raylene? He was going to do the same thing to Jonnie Coleman if we hadn't showed up, and it wasn't your neck his hands were around. He meant business."

Latice made a second plea. "We can just say we found him beat up on the street, brought him home, and then called the police."

"And what about when this bastard wakes up?" Gwena said. "Did you think about that? Somebody could get hurt."

Thelma added. "I'm already hurt, but I feel what Latice is saying. I say we take him and keep him, have a little fun while we're at it."

"Fun?" Gwena demanded. "Ladies, we are not sixteen talking about toilet-papering somebody's house. This is a human life we're talking about."

Raylene spoke through her shaking voice. "Latice, I think Gwena's got a valid point. Besides, this man is a monster. He's mean-spirited, violent, and like Gwena said, what you're talking about is against the law."

"No more against the law than hitting on women and running from the police." Latice's face was serious.

"Now that's what I'm talking about," Thelma said. She clambered to her feet. "Ladies, we all voiced our distaste with him at the last meeting, and I for one am not going to stand here and act like I didn't."

"I see your point," Gwena said. "But what you're talking about doing is ludicrous. Latice, just listen to what you're saying, please."

Latice stared at Gwena. "Yes, I hear myself. I hear myself *loud and clear,* and it's telling me to take the opportunity of a lifetime and include Second Pew. It's readers all over, readers like us that make the difference, and I'm sick and tired of the book industry and these little nappy-headed authors taking us for granted." Latice looked around and made her final argument. "We *all* should be tired. Damned tired."

Gwena was the only one who was not trying to be convinced. "Latice, you're an officer of the goddamned law," Gwena said. Her tone was now desperate and eager. "I would expect this from Thelma or maybe even myself, but not you."

Latice held her hands out. "I'm a parole officer," she said. "Not the police chief. Marcus needs some home training, so I say we give it to him."

"What?" Raylene asked.

"She's saying that we take him." Thelma was now on her feet and posted up against a Nissan. She wiped blood from her lip onto her sleeve. She looked at Latice. "I'm with it. This son of a cow owes me an apology anyway."

Gwena held up her hands. "Whoa. Let's not lose our heads. We are not *kidnapping* anybody. This man is hurt, and he doesn't know us from Adam. We need to set an example, do the right thing." Gwena spoke in a slow and articulate manner. "Raylene, put that cell phone to your ear right now, and call the police."

Raylene looked like a fat rat in between two cats, unable to make a decision on her own. "I can't. I can't choose."

"Then let's take a vote," Naomi offered. "Majority vote wins. If the vote is split we call the police. Agreed?"

Seeing the vote as a decent option, the women all agreed.

Latice looked around. These were the women she'd known at least the last seven years of her life. As the founding member of Second Pew, she remembered how they all met and hooked up. It had been Men's Sunday. The men were doing everything that Sunday, preaching, ushering, singing, cooking, and serving after-service supper. The church was so packed, they all ended up having to wait to be seated. By the time they were ushered in, the only space available was front and center on the second pew. And it was that day they clowned until service was over, and they discovered they'd all just finished reading *A Lesson before Dying*, by Ernest Gaines. Now here they were: Gwena and Raylene on one side, she and Thelma on the other while Naomi stood as stoic and unreadable as German physics to a three-year-old.

"Okay, all in favor of kidnapping Marcus Brooks, raise her hand."

Latice's hand and Thelma's hands flew straight up as they both looked around to see if they were alone. So far they were. The pressure was on.

Then as if an act of Congress had been initiated, Naomi's hand flew in the air, and it was over. By a three-two split, the book club was going to take the author.

"Naomi!" Raylene said. "How could you?"

Naomi shrugged. "I liked what Latice had to say, and I think we should do it."

"We're not thinking," Gwena said. "This is not smart at all."

"Where are we going to keep him?" Raylene asked as she used her hands dramatically to make her point.

"He can stay with us." Thelma cased the darkness. Voices were coming in their direction. "We need to hurry if we're going to do this."

"I have a pair of old handcuffs in my car. They're rusted but good," Latice said. "He can ride over in the backseat."

"But . . . ," Raylene stammered.

"Then it's settled," Thelma said. "We take him to my place,

hook him to the pipes underneath my kitchen sink, and commence to teaching him a lesson he'll *never* forget."

Gwena let out a sigh of pending defeat as she made a last plea. "I know *we* said *we* would never go against the vote, but can't we think about this?"

"Gwena," Latice said. "You're breaking the rule. We've already thought about it. The majority won."

She watched Gwena exhale, still not convinced. "The police are looking for him. That's one sign that we don't need to mess with this man." She looked around. "Am I the only one who thinks this is a bad idea?"

Latice walked over to Gwena. "Don't look at it that way," she said in her best persuasive voice. "Look at it as an opportunity to change the life of a very bad man."

Latice walked back over to where the author was lying. She reached down and began lifting him from the ground. "Now help me get him to the car."

MARCUS WOKE UP IN PAIN. His clothes had been removed, and he lay dressed in nothing but a T-shirt and his boxer briefs. His legs moved, and his toes and ankles felt fine, but the rest of him was saturated with pain.

The back of his head felt like it had been removed, and his face felt like it had been used for some kind of target practice. One of his eyes was slightly closed, his lips were swollen, and he felt a cut on his forehead.

From the looks of the pipes above his head he was on the floor in somebody's kitchen, underneath the sink. The cabinet doors had been removed, and anything previously stored in the cabinet was gone too. His hands were so tightly handcuffed that his wrists were sore and bruised. He could barely move his fingers.

He looked to his left on the wall of the cabinet and saw that his mother's picture had been removed from his satchel and frame and taped to the wood. Whoever had him at least had the decency to post his mother's photo where he could see it. Still, he wondered where he was.

The kitchen was old, like the one he grew up in. Everything considered major household appliance was in one room: the washer, dryer, oven, fridge, and freezer, but the appliances were modern. Whoever lived here was old-fashioned but had good taste. His stomach grumbled. The sound was so loud, a dog began barking from somewhere in the house. Marcus felt his fear heighten as the barks got closer. Soon a black dog came charging into the kitchen and up to him.

Marcus braced himself for the attack. The dog was huge, and even though the canine didn't bite him, it barked close enough to make Marcus painfully wiggle his way as far from the animal as possible, which wasn't anywhere far enough. He hated dogs. "Somebody come and get this mutt!" Marcus's voice was dry and cracked. "Hey!"

"Monroe, stop it," a female voice commanded the dog. The animal backed off.

When Marcus saw Gwena enter the kitchen, he didn't know whether to be angry, suspicious, or happy. He watched her retrieve a glass and pour some water. When she kneeled down by him offering the glass and two pills, he stared at her. "Please tell me I'm fucking dreaming," he said. "What? You didn't ruin my life enough in college?"

"Marcus, I know how this looks," Gwena said. "But I'm here to help you get out of this."

"Then unhook me from this goddamned sink if you want to help me," he said. "I should have known you were behind this shit." The look in her eyes longed for his calm and understanding, but Marcus wasn't trying to hear it. He was irate. "Are you going to sit there looking at me like I'm wrong, or are you going to give me the pills and water?"

She hurriedly offered him the water first. Marcus gulped the wetness down and emptied half the glass before he was ready to take the pills. The water felt cool going down. The tablets were tiny and pink, nothing remotely close to his usual packet of BC Powder.

Marcus frowned at them. "What kind of pills are those?"

"Something that will knock out the pain." She offered him the medication, but Marcus resisted. "They look like birth-control pills. Is this some kind of sick feminist move on the part of you and your coconspirators?"

"They are my book club members, and if you would just listen to me for once, you'd shut up so I can tell you how you can get out of this alive."

"Alive? Are you crazy? I'll be damned if I'm about to let an ex-bitch of a girlfriend and her dumb-ass book club bring me down." He cut his eyes from her. "And the last time I listened to you, I damned near got kicked out of school."

"Marcus, that was a long time ago. The book club is not going to tolerate you the way I did."

"Whatever, Gwena." Finally, tired of the pain, he looked at the pills. "Give them to me."

As she fed him the medicine and more water, Marcus stared at Gwena. After all these years, she was still one crazy bitch with good hair, nice skin, and an ass that just wouldn't stop. Too bad it had gone sour, because now he found her detestable. Gwena had done him dirty, and it was something he could forget only as long as she wasn't around.

"Marcus, you've been kidnapped," she said. "Raylene and Thelma are here with you today. Raylene isn't having much to do with you, so you have to depend mostly on Thelma. Don't piss her off."

Gwena retrieved a tube of ointment from the counter and rubbed it on Marcus's scrapes and bruises as she continued attempting to talk some sense into him. "Thelma had to go to work for an emergency around four this morning. She hasn't had much sleep and will probably be a little grumpy. Take my advice, and don't piss her off."

"Thelma?" he said. A bell went off in his head, and he remembered. She was the fighter. The one he'd almost rendered unconscious. "You mean to tell me y'all got this shit planned out?"

"Marcus, I need you to listen to me."

"What if I pay you ten grand to let me go?" he said.

"We don't want your money."

"Fuck you."

The pills were making him drowsy. Marcus fought the fatigue

as long as he could. "How'd you get your girls to follow along? What'd you tell them? That I raped you?"

She took in a breath. "Marcus, they don't know, and if you value your life, I'd advise you to chill." She wiped her hands clean and put lotion on them.

"I should have turned myself in."

"That's the one thing you've said that I agree with."

Marcus laughed long and slow. "Where am I?"

"Dallas."

Gwena always had a good sense of humor. It was the one thing about her that he could still appreciate. "Why am I being held?"

"You've pissed off a lot of women, including my book club."

"Book club?" Marcus laughed. "This is fucked up."

"I see you never learned to think before you spoke."

"And you never learned how to take it like a woman."

Gwena's hand covered his mouth. "I'm warning you." Her hand smelled sweet, like almonds and cake. "You're being held because we believe you can do better than write a book called *Bitches*." She slowly pulled her hand away.

"What is that supposed to mean?" Marcus had to hear this. He wasn't sure if Gwena was serious or not, but he'd play along just to get information.

"It means that you will not be released from here until you write another book to take the place of *Bitches*. That's all we want."

"We?" Marcus asked. "I thought you were on my side."

"I said I wanted to help you. I never said I was on your side." Gwena double-checked her shoes. "Just because I feel sorry for you doesn't mean I feel anything else."

"Don't flatter yourself." Marcus thought for a minute as he stared at Gwena from his good eye. "Rewriting a book is a lot of work."

"You can do it. The way you bragged about it on the *Lamont Troy Show*, I would think you really can write a book in your sleep." Gwena smiled a hopeful grin. "Besides, think of what you might really discover about yourself. A new book with a fresher outlook on relationships from you could only be beneficial."

"And what if I don't?"

She looked away. Uncertainty filled her face. "I don't know. That's why I'm trying to tell you to go with the flow."

"You've got to be kidding me," Marcus said. He thought for a second as he adjusted himself on the makeshift air mattress he was lying on.

"What day is it?"

"Sunday."

He'd been out well over twenty-four hours.

"Whose house is this?"

"Thelma's."

"Are the police still looking for me?"

"Yes."

"Good," he said in an attempt to intimidate her. "They'll catch you and rescue me."

"They don't have a clue where you might be," Gwena said. "Besides, after you clowned the way you did Friday, I doubt if finding you is at the top of their list of to do's."

"What about my stuff? Where's my satchel?"

"In Thelma's room." Gwena smiled. "I got your mother's picture out and taped it to the cabinet wall. I remembered that's how you liked to wake up."

"Bitch, I don't care what you remembered." He spat. "This ain't Let's Be Friends Day." He raised his knees to get some circulation running through them. "I need to make a phone call."

"No can do."

"Why not?"

"It's just one of the rules we have. No phone until you have some pages done."

Marcus lay there thinking. "I ain't rewriting shit."

"Fine. Have it your way. I'll let them deal with you. Maybe you'll finally be ready to listen to me and believe me when I say that I'm here to help." She rose and put the glass in the sink. "Just remember what I said about Thelma. Don't piss her off."

"Where are you going?"

Gwena looked at her watch. "Work."

"When I get out of here, I'm going to put a hurting on you much worse than I did in college."

Gwena laughed it off. "Who says you're getting out of here?" She picked up her keys and left.

Marcus watched Gwena leave the kitchen. As the pills took to his system, his eyelids become stones. He wasn't trying to fall for Gwena's game. After what she did to him in college, there was no way on earth he was going to play buddy to her now, and taking her advice was the last thing he was going to do.

THELMA'S EYE WAS COMPLETELY SWOLLEN and closed as she examined it in the mirror. The damage wasn't an emergency matter; she'd just be wearing shades for the next few days.

She'd grown up fighting. Back in Mississippi, with a mother who constantly raised hell wherever she went, fighting came natural. Not to mention, Arnise Wade was the single mother of eight daughters who were all just as unpredictable, tough, and defensive as their mother. Thelma was the fourth child and the only one not to go to law school *and finish*. Wade, Wade & Wade was the most successful family-owned law firm in Jacksonville, but Thelma wanted no part of it. Her love was medicine and animals, so she finished high school and did what no other Wade girl would do. She headed to the University of Texas at Austin, where she spent the next eight years studying animal medicine. When she finished and was ready to find a position, she moved to Dallas, where she'd been ever since. Thelma was the black sheep of her family, but still a fighter.

She brushed her teeth, pissed that she'd let Marcus hit her in the eye. Too many times she'd used the bob left, weave, bob right, and it had worked—but Marcus seemed to be somewhat of a challenge in that he got some lucky punches in.

She rinsed, did the mouthwash thing, and headed to the kitchen, where her nemesis and breakfast shared a room. Thelma loved to eat. If it weren't for her vegetarian lifestyle, she didn't think she would have the shapely frame or clear skin. She was built like a stone tower with the looks of a modern-day Jayne Kennedy, just not today. On this day, she had a black eye and bruises that dulled her model looks.

When she entered, the kitchen was quiet. She could hear Marcus's snores coming from beneath the cabinet. She stepped inside, flipped on the light switch, and began her day as usual. Her house slippers sloshed across the floor, the sound of getting pots and pans out to cook with was nothing short of junkyard-band loud.

"Hey! I can't sleep with all the noise," Marcus complained.

Thelma continued to slosh across the floor never-minding that it woke the author up. The more noise the better. She slammed the pots on the stove top and purposely sloshed over to the fridge, where she snatched the door open to get out some cooking ingredients. Soy scrambled eggs with soy sausage and soy milk for her wheat pancakes. As she crossed over Marcus, an egg accidentally fell on top of him, splattering yolk across his undershirt. "Godammit!" he yelled. "Hey!"

Thelma looked down. "It's just a little egg. Stop whining. I'll take care of it in a minute."

"I'm not going to let you treat me like I'm some nigga off the street. You better get over here and clean me up."

"I know one thing; you better watch who you talk to with that attitude." Thelma placed the food on the cabinet. When her hands were free, she kneeled down and pinched him three times hard and fast. Marcus yowled with each narrow grab of his skin. "I said I would clean you up in a minute and I will, you got it?"

Marcus said nothing. He looked like a kid terrified of an impending spanking. Then his stomach growled. The sound made Monroe bark from somewhere in the house. Thelma concentrated on getting the cooking done.

"That dog isn't coming back, is he?" Marcus asked.

"He's in my room with the door closed," Thelma said. Once she had everything cooking, she wet a dish towel and wiped up the egg. She had to remove Marcus's shirt, and when she saw how cut he was, a wave of butterflies forced her to turn away before he could sense her slight but obvious attraction to his six-pack and chocolate skin. She even liked the way his hairs crept up from his belly along the rim of his boxers.

"Your eye looks pretty bad," he said.

"So does yours."

"Yeah, but mine ain't closed." He licked over his cut lip and laughed.

"Isn't." She corrected him.

"Whatever."

Thelma was mad at herself for thinking such an asshole of a man could pique something inside her. As she stood at the sink, she grabbed her stomach to settle herself. She denied what she felt and subdued it, focused on sticking to the mission. Operation He Had It Coming was in full effect, and there was no room for mistakes.

When she tried to step across him to go to the fridge, he elevated his legs, stopping her. "You always been this fine?" he asked.

Thelma got smart. "God wouldn't have it any other way."

Marcus let out a whistle. "I could do a lot with a woman as fine as you."

"Should I be impressed?" She nudged him with her foot. "Because it ain't a damned thing I can do with a man like you except tie you up to keep you from ruining any more lives—now move your leg before I break it."

Marcus obeyed and lay there in quiet observation.

It wasn't long before the aroma of Thelma's cooking drifted through the house.

"Where'd you learn to fight like that?" he asked. He was trying to be polite, but for what, she didn't know and didn't care.

"Get out of my business."

"I was just trying to make conversation with you. Hell, I'm the hostage here—why are you being such a bitch?"

Thelma kicked Marcus in his ribs. "I don't know what kind of bitches you been messing with in the past, but I'm not one of them. You will respect me in my house or I'm going to kick the shit out of you again." She sloshed away from him and finished cooking.

When the food was done, Thelma sat near Marcus and prepared to feed him.

He frowned at the food. "What is that?"

"Breakfast?"

"No, I mean what is it?"

"It's a vegetarian omelet with wheat pancakes and rice."

"I'm a meat eater," Marcus said. "I want some sausage or bacon. Food for humans," he complained. "I can't eat this deer food."

"We don't eat meat in my house," Thelma said. "You'll eat what's in here or you *will* starve."

She offered him a spoonful of rice.

At first Marcus tried to hold out, but his stomach growled as soon as the smell hit his nose, and he couldn't resist. It wasn't long before he'd downed two helpings of his first vegetarian breakfast.

"That food is going to kill me," he said. "Tastes like something you'd give a dog."

"You'll learn to like it."

"I don't plan on being here that long," Marcus said. "This is some *Misery* type of shit that I can't get with."

Thelma cut her eyes at him. Standing up, he seemed a lot less threatening. She guessed it was because she could always see his eyes and practically know what he was thinking. "No, Marcus, because in *Misery,* the fan *loved* the author. In this case we don't like you or what you do." Thelma cleared her throat. "Then with that in mind, you should know that you won't be leaving here," she said. "Besides, Stephen King knows how to write. You don't."

"Tell my fans and my publisher that," Marcus's tone was bitter.

"I'm telling you!" Thelma yelled. Smart-ass mouths were one of her pet peeves, and Marcus had that department sewn shut.

He moved his lips to say something, but there was a certain look that Thelma was giving him that kept him from opening his mouth.

She offered him a glass of water when the doorbell rang. The sound made her jump, spilling water on Marcus's face and neck.

Thelma jumped to her feet as if an alarm had gone off.

Marcus choked. "Hey!"

Monroe barked.

"Can I have my pills before you get that?" he asked.

Thelma ignored his request. Instead she looked in one of the kitchen drawers and retrieved gray duct tape and scissors.

She kneeled again, cutting a piece long enough to secure his mouth. "If you so much as murmur through this tape, I'm going to put the heel of my foot on your nuts while my dog rips you apart. You got it?"

Marcus's eyes bucked. It was a sign to her that he valued his jewels and if he had to lose them, it wouldn't be because some woman stomped on them. He nodded in agreement.

Raylene came into the kitchen. Her hair was disheveled, and she looked like she hadn't slept in days.

"Expecting somebody?" she asked Thelma.

"No."

Thelma cut the tape. "Maybe it's one of the girls."

Raylene wrung her hands together. "What if it's not?"

"Raylene—" Thelma reinforced Marcus's mouth. "We won't know until we answer the damned door."

"What if it's the police?"

Thelma looked up. "Just keep your cool, Ray. Don't panic."

Raylene backed up and stood out of the way. Her facial expression was nothing short of terrified. She looked at Marcus. "What about him?"

"He'll be fine. Monroe'll watch him." Thelma called the dog into the kitchen, and at her command the dog lay with his mouth lowered near Marcus's jewels. "I'll stay in here while you get the door."

Raylene left the room.

Marcus began to scream through the tape. No sooner had he begun to complain, Monroe was on top of him lying on his sore ribs at Thelma's command.

RAYLENE OPENED THE FRONT DOOR, and there staring
back at her was Will, wearing a hangdog expression. He looked
pathetic, like a boy whose brand-new bike had been stolen. She
rolled her eyes. He was becoming a bugaboo, stopping by unex-
pectedly, calling all hours of the night and day, and sending her
flowers that she didn't ask for. Her room smelled and looked like
a botanical garden.

"Aren't you going to invite me in?" His voice was polite.

"No." She stepped out from behind the screen, putting herself
between the front door and Will.

"What's wrong with you?" Will searched her face. "Are you
already seeing someone else?"

"No, it's not that." She stumbled. "It's . . . just . . . the house is
a mess, and Thelma is not feeling well."

Raylene sat on the porch, looked out across Thelma's front
yard. The grass would need to be cut soon. She wondered if
Thelma had a lawn mower or if she called a lawn service. The
summer air was stiff, making the moment between her and Will
more excruciating. She wished they could go inside, but it wasn't
an option.

She pressed him. "What do you want—it's hot out here."

Will didn't move. "Then let's go inside, because I'm trying to
get your attention. I need you to talk to me."

"I already told you: Thelma isn't feeling well and the house is a mess." Lying to the man she was going to marry didn't seem so inconceivable to her anymore. His feelings for her were a lie.

"I don't mind. I'm not here to see Thelma or her mess." He wiped his forehead with a towel he pulled from his pocket. "It already feels like triple digits out here."

Her fiancé-in-question was right. It was hot. She could see the vapors from the sun's heat rising off the streets in invisible waves. She could stand to be in the air-conditioning of the house. Raylene jumped to her feet. "Okay, wait a minute. Let me clear it with Thel."

Raylene hurried into the house and closed the door behind her, locking it for extra precaution. Will was the kind of man who would walk in if she didn't lock the door.

Thelma was in the living room watching television. "Who was it?"

"It's Will. He's still here. He's outside on the porch and wants to come in."

Thelma looked around her. "Then let him in."

Raylene felt her mind begin to slip into a mild panic. "I already told him I couldn't let him in."

"Why not?"

"What if he sees or hears Marcus?"

"What if he starts snooping around because he feels like you're hiding something?"

Thelma did have a point.

"I'm sorry, but I panicked."

"Oh, God." Thelma jumped up. "It's not like you to be rude. Now he might suspect something. We have to act normal. Go let him in."

"I told him we were remodeling and that you weren't feeling well."

"You did what?" Thelma scratched her head. "Damn. Follow me to the garage."

She followed Thelma and watched her grab the few supplies she had, paintbrushes, trays, a tarp, and some Bubble Wrap that she had lying around. "Grab that set of sheets on the shelf behind you. Hurry."

Raylene followed Thelma's orders. The garage was smoldering, even with the door cracked. Her breathing felt constricted, but she wasn't sure if that was because of the heat or her quaking insides. She wanted to faint.

They scurried to the den and began moving furniture around. Raylene covered everything with the sheets while Thelma put the Bubble Wrap down, untidied her sofa, and threw a few empty water bottles around the room for added effect.

"You think it will work?" Raylene said as she wiped the sweat from her face and headed for the door.

"If it doesn't work, we'll just have to knock out Will and stick him under there next to Marcus."

Raylene gasped. The mere thought of having to tie up Will and hold him hostage made her uneasy. Thelma put Raylene's face between her hands. "Look, we're fine as long as he doesn't start acting nosy and walking around. You need to concern yourself with getting him out of this house." Thelma double-checked Raylene by wiping a sweaty hair from her face. "Calm down. It'll be okay."

Raylene watched her friend walk back to the living room before she returned to the door to invite Will in. He followed her to the sitting area in the ramshackle den, now with planted extras.

"You were right—this *is* a mess." He stood, not knowing where to sit. "I don't smell any paint."

"We have to border the walls with tape first."

"Oh."

Raylene was glad to see Thelma come into the den. She must have read Raylene's mind.

"Hey, Pastor." Thelma waved. She cut her eyes at Raylene and nodded for her to act normal. "Raylene, clear the couch so he can have a seat."

Will's face broke. "Jesus, what happened to you?"

Thelma smiled despite her bruises and closed eye. "Nothing, really."

"It doesn't look like nothing." Will walked up to get a closer look. "Did you get into a fight?"

"Actually, I'm an amateur boxer. I went to the ring yesterday and got in some practice."

"Good Lord," Will said. "I was just about to tell Raylene that I missed seeing you two at church today."

"We've been busy trying to redecorate. I figured since Raylene is an interior designer and living with me now, I could get twice the quality work done and help keep her mind off things. Besides, this face isn't going anywhere anytime soon." Thelma laughed. "I think I need to find another hobby."

"Sounds like a plan." Will found a place to sit and made himself comfortable. "Have you seen the news? The police are still looking for that author, Marcus Brooks."

Raylene's eyes bucked as she looked at Thelma. They'd been too busy holding Marcus Brooks hostage to watch the news. "Any new leads?"

"He checked out of his hotel, but missed his flight yesterday morning. The police say the trail runs cold from there. They suspect he's still in the city."

Raylene felt herself begin to swoon.

"Well, I hope the good Lord is watching over him." Thelma rubbed her neck in a calm fashion. "Don't get me wrong. I think the way he influences adults is sick and a sin. Marcus Brooks has no value system, and I for one hope that wherever he is he's finding out about values."

Will shook his head. "Amen, sister."

Raylene could see Thelma getting mad just talking about the author. She looked at her watch. "Thelma? Did you put the dinner rolls in the oven?"

Thelma rubbed her hands together as she caught on to the save. "I didn't, but I will go do that right now while we're taking a break. I'm going to let you two talk. Reverend, it was good seeing you."

"You too, Sister Wade, and I hope that eye of yours heals without any damage."

"Oh, I'm sure it will," Thelma said, and left the room.

"How are things at the house without me?"

"Lonely," Will admitted.

Raylene looked at Will, not sure if she should believe him.

They sat on the sheet-covered sofa that now stood in the middle of the room.

Raylene took a long look at Will. He was still attractive: almond skin, athletic build, bright smile, baby face. He was wearing the platinum diamond-encrusted cross she'd bought him two Christmases ago. The pendant shone against his skin. It was the first time she'd seen him with it on. She was still in love with the package. When they met, his looks were the first thing she noticed. It was a Singles' Ministry retreat in Little Rock, and all the single women had their eyes on the handsome new associate pastor who was being introduced, but he had his eyes on her. Will wooed Raylene hard that weekend, and within weeks they were a couple.

Will said he loved her because she embodied virtue and the light of the Holy Spirit. *That's what he said.* Now she understood what his description of her meant. Plain and simple, she was Will's trophy. She was the perfect preacher's wife in training. Pretty, smart, honest, Christian, and walking with blinders on. She hated to admit it, but that's what she was. She blinked away her thoughts. "I'm thinking of calling off our wedding."

Will sat up. "A week is hardly enough time to come to that kind of conclusion."

"Then give me a reason why I should not call it off."

"We haven't talked about it. You're making an emotional decision."

"I can't help my emotions." She'd raised her voice, something she said she wouldn't do. "I'm emotional, unlike you."

He threw his hands up in submission. "The Lord has been dealing with me. He's been speaking to me and telling me what to do."

"Did he also tell you to put your penis in Sister Henderson's mouth? Because if he did, I'm worshipping the wrong God."

Will scooted closer to Raylene. "No, he told me to take you to Jamaica. Just us two."

"Jamaica?" Jamaica was Raylene's favorite getaway spot, and she'd never turned down an opportunity to go.

She allowed his fingers to sink into the area above the nape of her neck. He began to massage gently. "We can dance in Kingston on the beach like we did the night I asked you to marry me."

"I could use the trip." Her voice was dreamy. "I miss the sand, fresh air, blue water. . . ."

Will's fingers chased the tension out of her neck. She missed his hands. She then let him kiss her earlobe as he whispered into her ear. "I can hold your body close to me, kiss you all night long on the white sand beaches, make up for this mistake I've made. You are my queen, my earth . . . my virtuous woman. I'll never let another woman touch me if you would just take me back."

Raylene was seeing herself wrapped in Will's arms underneath the blue skies of Jamaica until he brought up the reason why they would be going to Jamaica in the first place. She replayed the choir robe dick-sucking incident in her head before jumping out of his reach. "You had to go and say something stupid. You should have never done it in the first place."

Will let his frustration show. "Raylene, stop acting like people can't make mistakes. Nobody is perfect."

"We're not talking about perfection, here, Will. This conversation is about choices, and you made a choice against our union. I can't just ignore that."

From the kitchen Monroe began barking insanely.

Raylene froze.

"Is Monroe okay?"

"R-r-rats. We have rats. Big field-mice-looking rats." Raylene smoothed her hands over her pants. "They've been coming in from the garage. We caught a big one yesterday."

"I don't think I want you staying here if the conditions aren't . . . sanitary."

"Look who's talking. Will, I'm tired and I really can't do this right now. Why don't you come back some other time?"

He raised his sunglasses to get a better look at her. She must have looked tired, worried, or anxious. Maybe all three. "Are you okay?"

She nodded. "Just stressed."

"You wanna talk about it? I'm still all ears for you only." He gave her a playful push.

From the kitchen, Thelma began yelling at Monroe, but the dog's barks only ebbed into a continuous epic of growls.

Raylene held her face in her hands, looked into nowhere. She played around with the thought of telling Will about the kidnapping. "I've gotten myself in a pickle."

"What kind of pickle?" he asked. "Legal or not?"

Raylene let out a breath and got up quickly. "Never mind. It's nothing."

"Baby, it doesn't sound like nothing."

"Don't call me baby. Look, Will, you need to go. Your coming around here is just complicating things."

He stood, wrapped his arm around her shoulder, and massaged his thumb against her skin. "If you want to talk about it, call me, but please don't call off the wedding. We were meant to be."

Raylene didn't fight stepping away. His arms felt good around her. This time the words warmed her insides. The temporary comfort of his embrace made her want to forget everything, but the betrayal was all too fresh. They walked to the front door.

He released his hold, reached into his back pocket, withdrew a plane ticket, and put it in her hands. "And if you want to talk about *us,* meet me at the airport next Sunday."

Raylene watched him leave the house and walk down the sidewalk. This time before he drove off, Will honked the horn and waved. She returned the favor and walked inside.

"Everything okay?" Thelma turned from the television. Venus Williams was being interviewed. She'd moved on from tennis and wasn't winning like she used to, but she was okay with it.

"Yes and no." Raylene flopped on the love seat next to her friend. She waved the ticket between her fingers. "He brought me a plane ticket to Jamaica . . . says he wants to talk."

"Jamaica," Thelma replied heavily. "He's pulling out all the stops to get you back where he had you."

"But I love Jamaica. This ticket had to have cost him at least twelve hundred this time of season."

"I have to give it to him: he's doing all the right things."

"I know." Raylene bit her bottom lip. Holding the ticket was like holding the answer to sudden happiness. "I could get some thinking done if I went."

"Paradise isn't for thinking, Raylene. It's for fucking and getting played. And a man with a mistake on his conscience knows this, so don't get it twisted. Will just has the power and money to take larger risks in the name of saving his own reputation." Thelma nestled into the corner of the couch and kicked her legs up. "You sure can act naive when you want to."

"Girl, I'm thinking about beaches, blue water, and banana chips. I wouldn't pay Will any attention."

"Don't lie."

"I'm not."

"Then go ahead. If you think you're strong enough to be romping around in Jamaica free of charge with a fine man who footed the bill on a last-minute desperate attempt to get you back, then who am I to stop you?" She sucked her teeth. "Just don't be mad when you come back frustrated that you even went." Then Thelma swatted the thought away. "But what do I know? Hell, I don't even have a man." She laughed.

"But you never complain." Raylene laughed. "I've never seen somebody so content with being single. How do you do it?"

Thelma smiled. "How do you *not* do it? I enjoy my freedom."

Raylene thought. From the time she could remember, Raylene wanted to be happily married in a secure relationship with a man who loved her. Being in a relationship was what she strived for, and she assumed all women wanted to be in love until she met Thelma.

"I like the ideal of love and what it stands for between two people." Why was she defending herself? Why was it important for Thelma to see things her way? "That's how it's supposed to be. Women are supposed to be married. It's the way God planned it."

"Did God plan for you to walk in on Will and Fe Henderson and for you to turn right around and still become his wife?"

Raylene shook her head. That was one question she couldn't answer right away, but she knew she still believed in love and that there was someone out there who wanted to wake up to her and her only each morning for the rest of his life.

That was the reason she'd never given up on having boyfriends in high school and even in college, she'd dated hopelessly in search of real love, romance, and companionship. One guy in particular she still thought about occasionally. Greg Alston. He was her first everything, but his inability to deal with his family issues with his mother kept them from moving forward, and eventually the five-year, high-school-to-college relationship ended. With the exception of his cheating ways, Will reminded her of Greg, and that was a big part of her attraction to the minister. He was a really nice guy. At his core, he was genuine and could make her a five-course meal without coming up for air. Will was passionate too, but where Will seemed to borrow it, Greg was the kind of man that owned it.

"Too bad Will doesn't feel the same way," Thelma said. "Why spend your time looking for love when it's not looking for you?"

"Love *is* looking for me, and I'm not afraid to put myself out there to be found."

"But look at you. You're a bona fide mess behind love and romance. You might as well have my black eye." Thelma sat back and relaxed on the couch. "That's why I just play the field. Keep it open to protect myself."

"Thelma, don't you want to be romanced?"

"For what?" Thelma pouted her lips as if a brief-but-foul odor passed under it. "Romance is a fantasy. All I want is a little companionship and sex every now and then, but even that, I sacrifice sometimes for peace of mind. Maybe men and women weren't meant to be together. Shit, it's already been written that men and women aren't from the same planet."

"And I guess women and dogs are?"

"Monroe suits me fine. He listens, he cuddles, he protects. There are no sexual demands, and he obeys."

"But don't you want kids? Monroe can't be a father or husband. He can't even let himself out the house without you."

"No, I don't want kids. I can't run the risk of having a man's babies and then he walks away, leaving me with a bunch of his DNA transplants."

Raylene laughed. "Children are not transplants."

"Yes, they are," Thelma continued. "When we start talking genetics, I really get selective. The last thing I want is a fool for a baby's daddy. I don't think the trouble we go through to get a man is worth it, so I just say no. The men I select are single with big Johnsons and rhythm. That's all the man I can stand. You should try it sometime."

"No thanks." Raylene shook her head. "I just wish Will didn't have the desire to cheat in his heart. If I cheated on Will, he would go nuts."

"Then why don't you?"

"Why don't I what? Cheat?" The thought stirred something inside her that made her giggle.

"Yeah. Give that bastard a taste of his own hypocrisy." Thelma wasn't laughing.

"Thelma, I couldn't do that."

"Why not? Let that fool walk in and see you getting your swerve on."

"My swerve?"

"Sexed . . . let him walk in and see you getting sexed." Thelma huffed. "Raylene, sometimes I swear you can act clueless."

Raylene's mind went back to Greg. They'd kept in touch off and on, here and there, but she hadn't heard from him in well over seven years. She wasn't even sure if he was still in the United States.

Last time they talked, he was going to France to visit his parents. He would be the perfect man to cheat with . . . if she decided to cheat. She contemplated getting out the phone book and looking Greg up. If he was still in Dallas, she knew how to find him. If not, she knew where his father lived. She couldn't do that, could she?

"No. It wouldn't be right," she finally admitted.

Thelma exhaled loudly. "Get a little excitement going on in your life. Girl, once you free yourself from engagements, courtships, and looking for a love that don't exist, you'll see there's more to life than settling down. It's an option not a mandate. You liberate yourself."

Raylene looked at Thelma as if she were talking out of the side of her neck. "How can cheating be liberating?"

"Because it frees you from the sense of territory and ownership. Men don't like feeling like property, so why should we?"

"What? You're talking crazy."

"Fine. What works for me may not be for you. I can respect that."

Raylene was lost. Thelma was talking that feminist yang, and she didn't want to hear it. "Look, I'm not cheating on Will, and I'm not a piece of property." She blared, "You sound like that fool in the kitchen."

Raylene thought about Marcus. "Speaking of which, what did he do to make Monroe bark like that?"

"I'm not sure, but he's quiet now, which means he won't be making any noise anytime soon."

Raylene got up and peeked in on Marcus. She stood in the entrance between the kitchen and living room.

The author was still on the floor with his mouth taped. His face was dripping sweat, and Raylene could feel him angrily watching her.

Monroe lay nearby on his red, plaid, goose-feather pillow bed with a mahogany base. Thelma had had it custom-made. She spoiled him. The dog growled, forcing Marcus to close his eyes and pretend to be asleep.

Once again, she thought Thelma needed a consistent man in her life regardless of her antirelationship point of view. Thelma was pretty, smart, talented, and the only veterinary medicine specialist in Dallas who just happened to be a black woman. She had a lot going for her.

"Could you slide him some aspirin for me?" Thelma asked. "I've put some special painkillers on the countertop."

"Sure." Raylene removed her lean frame from the entrance panel and walked into the kitchen. She could feel Marcus's floorview glare follow her around the room.

Raylene walked over to the author and ripped the tape from his mouth.

"Why don't you just spit in my eye!" he said. "That shit hurt."

"My bad."

"And the next time you trifling nags decide to feed me, do it after I take my aspirin? Got it? Remember, I'm the victim here!"

He had some nerve talking smack, but Raylene had Jamaica, among other things, on her mind. She fed him the pills and water.

He swallowed until the glass was empty. "More," he said. "I'm dehydrated. My body is not used to going without water."

Raylene had to admit, he was ruggedly fit, modest on the chest hair, toned, rippled in the abs, and had a well-chiseled face. Nothing about him was unattractive except maybe his crooked bottom teeth and his pug nose that now sweated on the bridge.

"When do I get a bath?" He nestled back on the icepack, let out a satisfied sigh, and farted. "Which one of you lucky ladies gets to wash my nuts?"

Raylene was caught off guard by the comment and the sound of his flatulence. Her nostrils constricted. "Now see, that wasn't called for, you nasty insane man. You're not making this any easier on us by being disgusting."

"You're a mindless bleeding heart with book sense but no common sense. The perfect trophy wrapped in a nice tan. I see what preacher man likes in you. If you weren't such a fucking prude, I'd probably show you some respect," he said.

"You were eavesdropping on my conversation?"

"My mouth was covered, not my ears, and you and your preacher man don't whisper when you talk." His muscles began to feel like butter melting. Marcus relaxed.

"It was none of your business."

"What exactly happened between you two?"

Raylene made water for the dishes. Thelma was relentlessly old school and didn't even own a dishwasher, saying a machine that washed dishes was a second-rate idea, compared to diligent hands and sturdy muscle. Raylene didn't mind answering Marcus's question, because all the blame was on Will. "I caught him in the church with his pants down carrying on with one of the ladies from the Partners in Prayer committee."

"First-time offender?"

"What?"

"Was it his first time cheating?"

She put the stopper in the drain, looked out the window over the sink into the backyard. "What does it matter? If he cheated, he cheated, right?"

"You women never cease to amaze me when it comes to us fellas. You don't really know nothing about us."

Raylene wasn't in the mood to be schooled on her personal situation. She knew men well enough to know that the one she had cheated, and that's all that mattered to her right now. "Then what do I need to know?"

"Men cheat for various reasons."

Raylene went off. "I don't want to hear about reasons." She snapped. "My fiancé cheated because he's low-down and dirty. How's that for a reason?"

Marcus laughed mockingly. "Don't act so typical. You don't believe that, do you?"

Raylene didn't answer. She didn't know what she believed about Will's philandering or men being territorial. She didn't care.

Marcus responded, "He probably cheated because you either nag him all the time and he got depressed, he's getting you back for some foul shit you did, or he was trying to sow the last of his royal oats before walking the plank of being bound to your boring ass for the rest of his life."

"I'm not boring."

"Would you have done it?"

"Done what?"

"Whatever the other woman did for him. Would you have done it?"

"No, because I have way more respect for myself."

"What's that have to do with pleasing your man?"

"You sound like him. Trying to say I had something to do with it."

"No, you *did* have something to do with it." Marcus crossed his feet. "Men don't *just* cheat."

"What makes you the expert?"

"I'm a man, and men like women who can balance their internal freak and saint at the same time." He cleared his throat and asked, "What about the other woman? What is she like?"

"What do you mean?"

"Tell me about her. What does she look like?"

"A turtle."

"What? Are you afraid to tell me what she looks like? Are you scared I will hear something that will make me say she's prettier than you?"

"No, I'm not afraid. She really looks like a turtle."

"Be real."

Raylene inhaled. "She's shorter than me, average looking, with dreadlocks and a flat butt. She's nothing like me. I'm a way better package." Thinking of Sister Henderson only fueled Raylene's fire. "She calls herself a Christian, but there's nothing Christian about her."

"Then why didn't you check her?" Marcus asked. "She obviously doesn't have you beat in the looks department."

She quickly pulled her hands out of the dishwater and rested them on the sink's edge. "That's not my job."

"How's your sex life?"

"For your information, Will and I are . . . were practicing celibacy until the wedding day."

"Is he your man or isn't he? Do you believe God sent him to you or not?" Marcus's question hung in the air, waiting for Raylene to say something. "You don't cut a man off from something like that—you don't stop being real in the name of tradition or making it official. He's bound to find his satisfaction elsewhere."

She put her hands back into the water. Yes, Will was her man, and she felt God had sent him to her, but he'd ruined what they had, so Raylene felt no responsibility whatsoever. "Shut up, Mr. Brooks. This conversation is over."

"Go ahead," he said with a laugh. "Run from the truth."

"I'm not running," Raylene snapped under her breath. "Let's get that straight right now. I have morals, and Will knew that going into our relationship."

"The infamous inability of a woman to deal with the truth. No man is going to be denied sexual pleasure unless he's pussy-whipped, a eunuch, or waiting for something to clear up."

"Or a masochist handcuffed under a sink," she spat back. Raylene resumed washing the dishes without any more words between her and the author. She wasn't about to listen to an obnoxious, self-centered narcissist like Marcus Brooks.

Instead, she let her mind rest on getting away from him, and she had just the plane ticket to do it. Raylene had silently decided right then and there that she was going to Jamaica. Forget what Thelma or Marcus had to say. She had nothing to do with Will's stupidity, and she wasn't about to admit fault. And she would do them one better by stepping outside of her box tonight. This evening, Raylene would do the un-Raylene-able, even though in this moment, she didn't know what that consisted of.

MARCUS WAS BOUND to a chair and sitting upright the next time he woke up. However, his hands were still cuffed, and his feet were tied with both rope and gray duct tape. The pain in his head was numbed, and only a few of his bones still ached. The swelling in his lip was down, but a scab had formed over the cut.

No one was in the kitchen with him, but in front of him on the table was a laptop computer and a printer plugged in, turned on, and ready to go. The cursor on the screen blinked at him. He touched the keys. Maybe he should listen to Gwena? he thought as he pondered getting out of this situation alive. He'd just write some bullshit, use it as his opportunity to figure his way out.

When Marcus looked up, he saw two women staring back at him. One was Thelma, and the other was . . . he didn't know, but she was fat, and he remembered her from Friday night. She was the woman in the black dress. But, today she wore a security-looking outfit, blue blazer, white blouse, khakis, and gun holster that carried a nine-millimeter handgun. Marcus would love to get his hands on that, maybe bust a couple of caps in someone's ass before he went to the police and reported these loony tunes to the police.

"Who are you, Cagney or Lacey?" He laughed. "Or better yet, is that thing even loaded?" For a moment, Marcus felt himself lose it, and his weak laugh sounded like that of a madman.

The woman stepped into the room. "Mr. Brooks, I'm Latice

Harris, and as much as I hate to tell you, my son looks up to you. You influence him."

"So." Marcus sucked his teeth. "What's the fucking problem?"

Latice sat at the table with him. She gently touched Marcus's hand. "The problem is you're a bad influence."

He jerked away. "Don't you monitor what your son reads?"

"He's seventeen. He's old enough to choose what he reads on his own."

"So I ask you again," Marcus said, *"what's the fucking problem?"*

Thelma slapped him so hard, Marcus's neck popped. "You know what the problem is!" she said. "And if I have to tell you, then it's not going to be a very happy camp around here. I don't feel sorry for you. Listen to what Latice is saying."

Marcus flexed his jaw, making sure no internal damage had been done. "Okay," he whined out in pain. "I'm a bad influence and what?"

"Well . . . it would be nice if you would write a book that is not as offensive as this book everyone is talking about."

"Look, it takes a lot to come up with an entirely different work," Marcus said. "Why don't I just write your son a nice little short story?"

Wearing a low-cut red top that accentuated her plump breasts and solid neckline, Thelma sat on the other side of Marcus. "That's not going to cut it," she said. "You don't understand—we want a book to replace *Bitches*."

Marcus sucked his teeth. "No can do."

Latice got up and went to the fridge.

"Don't you think you've had enough of going in there?" Marcus laughed. "Your fat ass should be running away from the fridge, not walking."

Whack!

Thelma's hands were quick. "Say something else disrespectful, and I'm going to torture you in ways unimaginable." *Whack!* The second time, Marcus's face felt like it was on fire.

"Thelma, don't." Latice said. "Mr. Brooks, why do you feel the need to insult?"

"I don't feel the need. I just call it how I see it. Don't tell me you would disagree that you're fat . . . I mean . . . that you could stand to lose some weight."

Latice poured herself a glass of water and leaned against the counter. "I could stand to lose some weight, but I don't need you telling me."

"Well, somebody needs to," he remarked. "You have a nice face, but no man is going to deal with the rest of you."

Latice smiled. "A breakthrough. Did I just hear a compliment?"

Marcus sighed. "It's the truth, but so is the fact that you're fat."

Thelma twisted her lips. "How you ever made it this far, I don't know."

Marcus sat back in the chair. "I started out self-published. Sold books out of the trunk of my car wherever I could. I did what I had to do."

"So you're not a real author."

He looked at Latice. "What do you mean? I wrote a book that made it to the mainstream. Of course I'm a real author."

"But I mean you didn't go to school for writing."

"I have a degree in journalism—it's enough. You don't need a writing degree to write."

Thelma sucked her teeth. "But you do need to know how to write, which you haven't done since *From the Palm of My Hand.*"

Marcus laughed. "You book club women think you have it all figured out, and you don't know nothing. You have no idea what it takes to sit down and compose a story. You have no idea what authors go through to please your picky asses."

"We know enough," Latice said. "If it weren't for us, half of you ignorant-ass authors wouldn't exist in the mainstream."

"Yeah, and if weren't for us, book clubs wouldn't exist. What would you get together for besides eating and basking in each other's misery?"

"Our book club is a friendship of sisters, Marcus. We don't

need authors like you around. As a matter of fact, we've only read one of your books as a group, so at this particular moment, you are expendable to us."

"Yeah, right." Marcus said. "I beg to differ."

Latice laughed. "Now that I think about it, Gwena didn't hit you hard enough."

"Who did you say hit me?" The comment had caught him off guard. Marcus stared at the chubby-cheeked middle-aged woman. The look on his face was already growing into a low frown.

"Gwena hit you," she said, laughing. "Like Babe Ruth in the final inning with bases loaded." The women busted out in laughter at Marcus's expense.

"She didn't mean to. As a matter of fact, she's the only one who is absolutely totally against this."

Marcus felt betrayed and lied to, even though he'd never known Gwena to lie. He'd given her the benefit of the doubt and found himself on the cracked end of the stick. Gwena was about to regret trying to pull the wool over his eyes. He was the wrong man to mess with, even in handcuffs.

He had enough information to give to the police if he could just get the women to free him of the cuffs. He gave a second thought to rewriting the book, but then thought against it. There was no way a bunch of women were going to come along and try to control his life. It was time for Marcus to represent brothers everywhere by using his brain, courage, and strength to get the hell out of his situation and have these females locked up. The national coverage would boost his career ten times over. He'd be a made man.

The swelling in his wrists had gone down, but it still hurt when he pulled against the cuffs. He gave himself a few more hours before he would have the actual strength to regain his freedom. Until then, divide and conquer would have to do.

"Gwena's got all of you fooled."

"What are you talking about?" Thelma asked.

"Gwena and I went to college together."

Latice and Thelma fell quiet. Latice's gaze was probing while Thelma's remained distant and uninterested, but he knew he had their attention.

Marcus continued to gamble. "She almost had me put out of school."

"You went to Southern?" Latice asked as if stumped.

"Jaguar till I die, baby," Marcus bragged. "We were there together."

The I-didn't-know frown on Latice's face told all. "That's a lie. If Gwena went to school with you, we'd know."

"Maybe you weren't supposed to know. What if she didn't want you to know?"

Thelma pounded the table. "Prove it."

Marcus folded his hands in front of him. "Gwena Nicole Phelps was homecoming queen, she graduated with a degree in broadcasting, and she did some acting while at Southern."

Thelma chimed in. "Where did she stay?"

"MacGregor View apartments."

"What is her sister's name?"

"Gwena is an only child."

"How did Gwena almost have you put out of school?" Latice asked.

"She said I raped her."

Silence sliced through the three of them.

Marcus was on point.

"Why should we believe you?" Thelma asked.

"You don't have to. Just ask her," Marcus said. "Gwena Phelps was a lot of things, a fuck buddy, intense, delusional, and a bit on the selfish side, but never a liar." He knew that much to be true. All three of them did.

Thelma and Latice were now quiet again. Marcus had 'em. His divide-and-conquer scheme just might work.

"Why would Gwena want revenge?" Thelma lifted a cigarette from the pack sitting on the table.

"You shouldn't smoke," he said. "It makes you old before your time." Then Marcus crossed his outstretched legs. "I said the woman was delusional, didn't I?"

"Shut up and talk." Thelma lit the stick anyway. She inhaled and blew the smoke in his face.

Marcus knew not to push Thelma too far. She was quick to throw a punch and didn't seem to care that he was already in a bad way.

He popped his toes and told the story of what went down between him and their saintly book club member.

"Like I said, Gwena and I used to date, but we were into freaky stuff when it came to sex."

"Freaky stuff," Latice said. "What kind of freaky stuff?"

"Gwena was into bondage real heavy back then. She liked for me to tie her up, slap her on the ass, you know . . . pulling hair, scratching, deep throating, and anything else you can imagine. Well, this one night, she wanted to play this game that was pretty rough, but I agreed to it. At first it was all good until I pinned her arms behind her and basically took what I wanted. When it was over, she was crying and hysterical, saying I'd gone too far, and she reported it to the school. I was pulled out on rape charges."

"Sounds like rape to me," Latice said. "Sick."

"Marcus Brooks," Thelma said, "if this is a joke, I'm not laughing."

"Good," Marcus replied. "Because I'm not joking."

"What kind of game was it?" Latice asked.

Marcus looked at the women and had second thoughts. *Maybe Gwena is right and the women knowing will further endanger my life*. Gwena wasn't a liar. There was only one way he would know. Marcus wasn't afraid to find out. He was a man through and through, and nobody's semi-intelligent hoodlum from off the streets. "The Rape Game," he heard himself say. "She'd pulled the instructions off the Internet. That's how I walked away a free man, and it pissed her off. It's the truth. She's been lying to you, and I guarantee you that when it's all over, said and done with, you will go down for her sick plot at getting revenge. That's what this is."

He watched Thelma and Latice look at each other. Uncertainty shadowed their expressions.

Thelma removed the cigarette from her mouth and put it out. She got up from the table and walked out of the kitchen. "We'll talk to Gwena, but in the meanwhile, you have work to do."

He could tell she was unnerved by the story. Once they talked to Gwena, it would be a matter of hours before he was freed and able to get the hell out.

Heavy in thought, Latice tapped her fingers on the table. Marcus saw it as the perfect time for him to nail the stake in a little harder. "I'm sorry that your son happens to be a fan of mine, but maybe now is a good time to be sitting and talking to him instead of holding an innocent man hostage."

Latice cut her eyes over at Marcus. "I'm not Thelma. This bullshit story you've told don't cut right with me, and I believe Gwena will tell us the truth."

"And the same truth will set me free." Marcus put his hands on the computer keys. "Why don't you ladies leave me alone while I get to retyping. I need my privacy." Marcus smiled.

Latice left the kitchen. The woman's attempt at holding her head high was nothing more than a front. Marcus could see it written on her face as clear as day. She wasn't sure.

He'd told so much that shocked them, Gwena would have no choice but to come clean.

He smiled a deceitful thin-lipped grin. He had the women right where he wanted them: focused on each other and not on him. Now *he* could focus on escaping.

Suddenly Thelma stomped back into the room and rammed a needle in Marcus's arm. The pain felt like a pinch to his bone. He wailed out in horror. "What the fuck?"

"I'm putting your ass back on the floor!" she hollered, and then slammed the laptop closed. "Forget writing a book for now."

"No!" Marcus tried to fight it, but the medicine had his head rolling in no time. There would be no thinking about escaping tonight. Only dreams of dreams free.

Naomi hurriedly slid into a pair of open-toed clogs as she grabbed her duffel bag. Vincent was still sleep. She looked at her husband doing what he did best when he was home from touring. As a matter of fact, that's all he seemed to do, but this time, she wasn't making an issue out of it. She had more important things on her mind, like getting over to Thelma's for the emergency meeting before her shift started. She hoped the meeting wasn't about her, even though she could think of nothing she'd done wrong. She hoped the women were ready to surrender and release the author. Harboring him proved more stressful than she'd thought.

The boys were at their grandmother's house, and Naomi had made arrangements for them to stay the week so she and Vincent could spend some time alone. She grabbed Marcus's first book from the nightstand next to the bed. Vincent would get a small kick out of having it autographed. Maybe it would clear some of the tension between them. Her shuffling around woke him.

"Where are you going?"

Vincent's voice stirred her from her thoughts. "Thelma's. The book club is getting together."

"But you were together yesterday *and* Friday. Stay at home with me—let's take in a late movie or go have drinks and listen to some live music."

"I can't tonight, Vince. I promised Thelma I would come over and help her do some painting."

"You tossed and turned all night. Stay home and get some rest."

Vincent had no idea. She hadn't slept a wink in two days going on three. Naomi looked in the mirror, primped her weave removed, short flipped hairdo, put concealer on the bags under her eyes, applied some lip shiner, and double-checked her nose for uninvited green guests.

Vincent watched her from the bed.

She looked at him. Saw the love in his eyes. "Can I help you?" she asked in a coy and teasing voice.

"Yeah, come back over here and get in the bed with me. I want to hold you."

Naomi teased as she applied more gloss to her lips. "Let me think about it." The offer was tempting, but Naomi couldn't go against the vote. Thelma had called an emergency meeting, and she was already running late.

Vincent rolled over on his back and grabbed the remote. He went straight to the news. "I wonder if there are any updates on Marcus Brooks? The last news report said this might be foul play."

Naomi froze. Vincent had been keeping up with the author's disappearance. "He was last seen headed to Deep Ellum. One of those girls down there probably slid him something. Never know with all the clubs in that area."

Naomi turned the light off and sat on the bed. "They'll find him."

"I don't know, babe. That brother has a lot of enemies," Vincent said. "Women all over are protesting him. Someone could be out for his blood." Vincent cleared his throat and rubbed Naomi's back. "You got time for a quickie?"

Naomi looked at her watch. She hurried to her feet and began grabbing her things. "I have to go. We'll snuggle when I get back. I'll even give you a blow job."

He laughed under his breath. "So just forget about me, right? I haven't seen you in months, and the book club is more important than me. You try and pacify me with a blow job?"

"Are you saying you don't want it?" Naomi smiled playfully. Vincent couldn't be serious.

"I'm saying I'm tired of being put off to the side like I don't matter around here."

"Vince, you're overreacting." Naomi pouted. "Please understand. I *promised* Thelma that I would help her. I just want to keep my word."

"I understand," Vincent shot back. "You promise the goddamned book club time you're supposed to promise me."

"That's a selfish way to look at it," Naomi responded.

"And that's a selfish way to be," he said back. Naomi watched her husband fall back on his pillow. He stared at the television, deliberately ignoring her. "I'm going back on the road with Jill Scott at the end of the week."

Naomi halted. Her rich brown eyes searched her husband's face until he couldn't help but to look at her. Vincent wasn't supposed to be going back on the road for another month. It was only July. "When did this happen?"

"Jill's MD needs a lead guitar player for a small West Coast tour she's doing, and her people called me."

"And you just up and told them yes without so much as sharing it with me?"

"What does it matter?" The question was flippant. "Friday, I was in the way, and today I'm not even on the radar."

"We are still married, Vincent, and I'd appreciate a little consideration from you, that's all." She grabbed sunglasses, keys, and ChapStick off the dresser. "You don't get it."

"Get what?" Vincent sat up in the bed. His twists were beginning to 'fro out at the roots. Naomi was sure he'd have to have it done before he left. He scratched his chest. "Two days ago you didn't want me here, so what difference does it make now? I'm not good enough to be with my own kids. I'm not good enough for you to keep your friends out of my business.

I'm not even good enough to be appreciated for buying this house, paying the kids' tuition, keeping the yard mowed, or being your husband."

She gazed at him angrily, looking for a sign that Vincent was joking. "That's shit you're *supposed* to do," Naomi shot back. "Why should I thank you for what you should be doing?"

"You recognize the things I'm not doing, so why should my expectations be different? I might as well leave."

"Vince, I don't want you to leave, I just want you to—"

"Change?"

"That's not what I was going to say."

"What then? Be different?"

"I didn't say that."

"Not be myself?"

"Vince, don't put words in my mouth."

"Do things your way?"

"No, and stop interrupting me!"

Vincent sat up and muted the news. "That's all you didn't say, Naomi. You made it plain and clear that when I'm home, I need to fit in instead of just being who I am. I can't even be with my own kids without you telling me how to be. I'm sick of it."

"And I'm sick of you playing the victim!" Naomi shot back. "I'm sick and tired of feeling like I'm carrying ninety percent of the load around here. Vincent, your idea of being you is a lazy idea. I'm tired of coming home to shit like you watching Marcus Brooks on television as if he can somehow tell you something you don't already know. You waste your time when you're at home."

"Then why are we living in a four-hundred-thousand-dollar home if I'm lazy and waste my time?" Vincent scratched his five-o'clock shadow.

"Snuggle bunny, that's not what I meant."

"Save the terms of endearment for somebody who can be who *you* want them to be all the time. I'm the lazy man who works, spends time with his kids, and loves his wife more than life itself. You don't want to talk to me." Vincent threw the covers back, stepped out of the bed. "I want the woman who used to see the greatness in us despite my faults because she knew she had faults too."

"I'm still your wife, and this is not about faults, Vincent. This is about right and wrong."

"There is no right and wrong when it comes to how I'm choosing to be in my children's lives. You used to be happy with it." He looked at her before going to the bathroom. "I mean everything I say. I want my wife or another life!" He slammed the door.

She was past stunned, but she wasn't about to let Vincent's temper tantrum ruin her day. She would not argue with him. She had too much on her plate, too many other worries and responsibilities, to allow Vincent and his lack of common sense to impede her current commitment to Operation He Had It Coming. Naomi walked over to the bathroom door and knocked lightly. "I'll be back tonight, and then we can talk. Okay, Vince?"

There was no response from the other side.

Vincent was acting like a child, and she wasn't in the mood to deal with that kind of behavior this day. Naomi cleared her throat in a dignified manner. "Fine, be that way," she said. "We'll talk when I get back, I promise." Naomi touched the bathroom door, still hoping to get a response, but she couldn't wait all night. After getting no answer, she walked out of the room and hurriedly headed out.

When she pulled up to Thelma's house, Naomi felt a sense of relief come over her. She still refused to see things Vincent's way, because he was wrong and was being excessively selfish about helping her out. She took a breath, said a small prayer, and vowed to get things cleared up with her husband when she returned home.

Thelma was already at the door waiting. Her face had healed considerably in two days, but the swelling still shone around her eye, and her legs and arms were still skinned by the concrete.

"You're late."

"I know," she groaned. "Vincent and I had to go a few rounds before I could leave."

"What happened?"

Naomi thought about her husband's desire for privacy. "Nothing really." Her voice wavered. "As a matter of fact, it's not important enough to share."

Latice stood up. "Ladies, we need to talk."

"What about?" Raylene asked.

Thelma sat down. "It's about Gwena."

"Me?" Gwena asked. "What about me?"

Naomi looked around curiously. She glanced at both of the women who seemed to be squaring off.

Marcus began to yell at them from the kitchen for some water.

All eyes landed on Naomi.

"It's your shift," Raylene said. "I can't go in there anymore today."

Naomi slowly stood. "Don't anyone get up. I'll take care of it."

She walked into the kitchen. It was her first time seeing the author awake. Yesterday, when she stopped by, he had just been given painkillers that put him out.

Naomi kneeled where he could see her. He looked even more menacing up close, which made her glad he was handcuffed to the pipes. Next to him was a photo of a woman with enough facial hair to be called Harry. She could tell from the eyebrows and the way the woman's mouth was wide-set on her face that it was Marcus Brooks's mother. They looked more alike than different.

"Is that your mother?" Naomi asked.

"Yes, the only woman who ever loved me," Marcus bragged.

"I can see why." She found something else to look at. Marcus's mother looked like the bottom of a skillet.

"Damn, this is the finest book club I've ever seen in my life," Marcus said, unaware that Naomi was frowning at the photo.

"Except Latice, I'll let slide because she has a pretty face. Normally, I don't like fat women."

Naomi ignored Marcus. It was advice Latice had given them all, and rightfully so. He was a nonstop, foul-mouthed, chatterbox with too much machismo for his own good.

"You must be Naomi," he said. "I heard them say you were on your way, but they never said your *fine ass* was on your way."

She continued to ignore him as she filled the cup with filtered water from the sink. "I'm sure they don't like you either."

"Do all of you have smart mouths?"

She could feel him trying to keep his eyes on her as she crossed the floor to get a cup.

"Can I make a phone call?"

Still no response. Latice had given strict instructions on how to handle the author. Naomi knew all rules regarding the hostage had already been established. No phone calls, no e-mails sent out on his behalf, no talking about this to anyone, and under no circumstances should he be tolerated for bad behavior, which made ignoring him perfectly acceptable.

He obviously didn't care that she was ignoring him, because he kept talking. "I could do a lot with a small, round booty like yours. Smack it up, flip it, rub it down."

Naomi kneeled to give Marcus the water. As he prepared for the refreshment, she dashed it on him instead. The author was sent into a symphony of coughs and gags. His dirty shirt was now drenched, as was his face, which glistened with beads of water.

"What is your fucking problem?"

"You."

"Don't you know a compliment when you hear one?"

"I don't need you to tell me how fine I am. I have a husband for that, thank you." She rose to get more water, still feeling his eyes following her.

"Your old man must be weak. He can't even keep you at home."

"My husband is not a control freak. He's a gentleman, a wonderful father, and a great lover." She toted the glass over and retook her place by him on the floor.

"Then why are you here?" Marcus asked. "You should be at home, thanking him for being Mr. Wonderful instead of being here dealing with me and your insane girlfriends. Tell the truth, this wasn't your idea, was it?"

"Hush."

"Don't be afraid to talk to me. I can't do anything from under here."

Naomi fed him the water. "I don't need you telling me what to do. I take care of home. I know my husband and our sex life is none of your business."

"Your husband would probably tell me. We men talk about stuff like that, you know. He could be like Raylene's man, Right Honorable Pastor Robinson, right?"

"You should really mind your own business," she preached. "My husband is satisfied, and we don't need any pointers from you."

"Whatever," the author replied. "If you have to tell me, then it's probably not as tight as you think it is." He drank the water until it was all gone. "Your old man is probably at home right now regretting marrying such a know-it-all, self-righteous woman." He wiggled his toes. "If there's one thing a man hates, it's a know-it-all woman."

"You ever been married, Mr. Brooks?"

"No."

"I figured as much. You're talking about something you have no knowledge of." Naomi put the cup on the counter. However, she was thinking about Marcus's words. She and Vincent hadn't had sex since he'd been home this last time. She was hoping to make up for that while the kids were gone, but things had to be done in order. She didn't want to lose track or concentration on the bigger issue, which was the kidnapping. She made a mental note to make everything up to her husband after Wednesday, complete with some oral stimulation. It had been a while since

she'd given him any, but Naomi knew it was like riding a bike.
You never forgot.

Commotion erupted from the other room. Naomi could hear
Thelma and Gwena yelling back and forth. She got up to see what
was going on.

"Looks like the ship's starting to sink." Marcus got comfortable on the floor. "It's only a matter of time before you lonely,
violent, psychotic bitches get what's coming to you."

Naomi left Marcus to find Gwena and Thelma hollering at
each other. Latice stood between them like a referee, keeping
them separate with her outstretched arms, while Raylene sat on
the couch in wild-eyed awe.

G WENA WAS PREPARED to fight Thelma if she had to, although at the moment, all they were doing was exchanging harsh words. She removed her cap defensively. No one was going to get in her face to call her a liar or a bitch and get away with it.

Naomi walked into the room. "What is going on?"

Thelma angrily shouted, "Gwena lied to us!"

"Thelma, we don't know that," Latice said. "We need to let Gwena talk."

"I don't need to hear anything Ms. Phelps has to say," Thelma said.

"Lied about what?" Naomi asked.

"Everything," Raylene said. "She lied about everything."

"I did not lie to this book club!" Gwena said. "Just because I didn't tell you, it doesn't mean that I lied."

"Then what does it mean?" Raylene asked.

Gwena pointed at Ray. "Don't you even try to front me, Ray." Then she walked over to Naomi. "I knew Marcus Brooks from school," Gwena admitted for the second time that night. "He and I used to date, and there was once a time in my past when I accused him of raping me."

"Tell her how you let him pull on your hair and tie you up!" Thelma's tone was enraged.

Gwena cut her eyes at Thelma. "It's true. Marcus and I used to . . . engage in . . . violent sex acts."

Naomi's eyes bucked. "I can see how you didn't want to tell us that. But don't you think it was important for us to know this on Friday night?"

Thelma walked away and lit a cigarette. "For all we know, she's been planning this shit from jump. Second Pew was nothing but a pawn in her game. We've been tricked."

"Thelma, I'm warning you," Gwena said. "You may be bigger than me, but I will not stand here and let you accuse me of something I am not guilty of. I never meant for this to happen."

Thelma walked away. "That's bullshit, and you know it."

"Well," Raylene added. "You should have been honest from the get-go."

Latice looked at Gwena. "Did you have anything to do with the charges that Marcus has pending against him now?"

"No," Gwena said. "He doesn't even know I was at the television station. Not unless one of you have told him?"

Naomi paced the floor. "So who do we blame for this? Gwena or Latice?

"Me?" Latice shot around.

"Yes, you! You were the one talking about kidnapping the son of a bitch! Maybe this was all you and Gwena's plan."

Gwena closed her eyes and rubbed her forehead. "You've got to be kidding me."

The women erupted in a sea of yelling, finger-pointing, expletives, and name-calling.

Thelma had the most to say. "Maybe he doesn't know because Gwena knew if he saw her, then her chances of kidnapping him would fold."

Gwena was tired of Thelma's mouthing off. She sat long enough, taking the verbal abuse from a woman who didn't know what was going on. "I didn't lie. The only reason I never told you is because I'm over it and I've been over it for a long time now."

She let her weight rest on one hip. "If that was the case, I could have told you that Marcus was afraid of cockroaches and that he stutters when he's afraid, but I have no desire to denigrate him or get revenge. I'm not the one who instigated kidnapping him. This was never my idea!"

"That's true," Naomi said. "It was all Latice."

"We voted," Latice snapped at Naomi. "And the vote was *your* idea!"

"Who cares whose idea it was," Raylene yelled. "What are we going to do?"

"Quiet!" Gwena yelled.

The women went silent, and that's when they heard it. Marcus Brooks was in the kitchen laughing.

The women's heads fell in shame.

"He's pitted us against each other." Thelma walked over to Gwena. "Look, it doesn't matter. What happened between you and Marcus is in the past."

"Thank you." They hugged.

Raylene walked over and joined in the embrace.

Naomi and Latice followed suit.

"United we stand; divided we fall," Latice said. "We have to stay united."

Raylene scratched her head. "So what are we going to do?"

"I say we turn him in and tell them we did it because we found out we were being used." Naomi was the first to speak.

"Thank God you've finally come to your senses," Gwena said. "At first I asked Marcus not to say anything, but now, I'm glad he did. And for your information, I didn't *use* anybody."

"No," Latice said. "There's still one unanswered question."

"What?" Gwena felt her heart begin to race.

"Did he or didn't he rape you?"

Gwena shrugged. "He did, but a court of law says he didn't. I was angry about it for a long time, but not anymore. It was my own fault for being promiscuous anyway. I've learned my lesson."

Gwena felt all tension leave the room. "I'm not ashamed to admit that yes, I used to get down real heavy when I was in college, and yes, Marcus and I had a thing, but the night we played the game, he turned into a madman. He crossed the line."

"Hell, it was the Rape Game," Thelma said. "I can hardly see us having this conversation about you two playing Monopoly or Trivial Pursuit."

Gwena sighed. "Unfortunately I had to learn the hard way that my body is a temple for life and not experimentation. I'm at peace with it, and I've moved on."

"I wonder if Will believes his body is a temple?" Raylene huffed. Then she chimed in, "Bastard."

Thelma laughed. "Uh-oh . . . somebody's finally starting to show some anger around here. There is life on Venus."

Raylene rested her head on the couch. "Fuck Will," she said. She looked up, as if surprised that the words had come out of her mouth. "There's nothing he can do or say to make me deny what I saw last Sunday. I can't let it go."

"It's called values," Latice said. "And I won't get over what I saw either."

Raylene looked around, letting her eyes finally fall on Gwena. "I believe you and I don't think we should let Marcus Brooks go anywhere."

"That's the spirit!" Latice said.

Gwena frowned. "But—but that's not—what I meant to—"

"You know what?" Thelma said. "The girls are right. We made this decision as a book club, and I say we see it through as a book club."

Raylene grabbed Gwena and pulled her in. "We're not going to let something that had nothing to do with us break the vote. Nothing breaks the vote. United we stand; divided we fall." Raylene's speaking up caught everyone off guard.

Gwena inhaled and let out a half-laugh. Her tone quieted the room. "Ladies, I'd rather not hang around anymore." After a pause, she spoke again. "Don't be mad," Gwena said. "I didn't want to have anything to do with this in the first place, and being in this position has almost ruined seven years of therapy for me." Gwena left the circle and grabbed her things. "I can't do this right now. I'm breaking the vote. Consider this meeting over."

Gwena walked out the door, leaving the Second Pew Book Club and Marcus Brooks behind her.

LATICE'S ANGER AT MARCUS showed. She marched into the kitchen after Gwena left. She used her motherly force, and put her foot on his ribcage, knowing the pain it caused.

"Get off me!" Marcus said through clenched teeth. His morning breath was two days old, and now he smelled, but there was fight left in him, a fight Latice wanted to tame.

She began searching the cabinets.

"Latice, what are you looking for?" Raylene asked.

"A jar."

"There's one in the cabinet over the stove," Thelma said.

The three women stood in the doorway, watching Latice.

"I need to piss," Marcus said.

"I'm not doing it this time," Thelma said. She pointed at the bucket in the corner behind the back door. "Any volunteers?"

"Don't worry about it. Leave him there, and don't touch him," Latice said. "I'll be right back." She took the jar and headed out the front door.

When she returned, Naomi was waiting for her. "Where have you been? We almost called the police."

"Naomi, stand back," Latice said. The jar was hidden in her purse, and she wasn't going to pull it out until the timing was right. She stepped back into the kitchen.

"I need to make a phone call," Marcus said. "Right now."

Latice sat down and looked at him. "The only person you'll be calling is Jesus when I'm through with you."

Marcus's eyes darted from Latice's to the others surrounding her. "Where's Gwena?" he asked.

"She's gone," Latice said. "When we confronted her about what happened, she left. You ran off the one person that wanted to help you."

Marcus let out a nervous smile. "So, you're letting me go, right?"

"Wrong," Latice said.

"But I thought you said she left?" he said. "Shame and guilt was too much for her to handle . . . right?" The grin that once brightened his face was now gone.

"Wrong again," Latice said. "Gwena doesn't want to have anything to do with you, and even though it's true that you and Gwena had wild sex and played something as stupid as a rape game, I can't get over the fact that you even wanted us to know that about you. I'm ashamed, disgraced, enraged, and I think it's time to change some attitudes around here."

"The feeling is mutual," Marcus said. "And when I get out of here, I'm not ever coming back to Dallas."

Latice pulled the jar from her purse. The few cockroaches that crawled around in the jar made the author's eyes buck in fear.

"What . . . are . . . you planning to do with those?" he asked. Tears raced from the corners of his eyes down the sides of his face, coursing to his neck.

"I'm going to pour them on you if we don't start getting some cooperation around here, understood?"

Suddenly a large wet spot appeared on the front of Marcus's boxers. He was peeing on himself. "Yes!" he said. "I understand."

Naomi and Raylene reeled back in disgust.

Latice set the jar right by Marcus long enough to watch him squirm, and then she placed it back in her purse.

Thelma stood in the door, her nostrils contracting reflexively.

Naomi stared down on him, her lips bunched up to her nose. "You stink for real now," she said.

Marcus immediately became upset at the embarrassing scene. "When I get out of here, I'm going to make sure none of you sorry bitches see light of day again!"

Latice put her finger in his face. "*You* won't see light of day again if you don't get it in your head that this isn't a game, and the next time you try some tired shit like divide and conquer, you better be ready to be divided and conquered."

Raylene looked at her watch and rubbed her eyes. "It's after ten. We need to close this out." She yawned and stretched.

"What's your rush?" Latice asked. "Going somewhere?"

"No," Raylene replied. "But tonight is Thelma's shift, and for once I can get in the bed before midnight."

"I need to get home to my husband anyway," Naomi said. "I'll see you ladies tomorrow."

The two left, leaving Latice and Thelma to see over a now pissy-smelling Marcus.

Marcus shook against the pallet. "I need a bath!" he yelled.

Latice stood and fixed her purse on her shoulder. She glanced at Thelma. "I'll let that be your decision. If you need my help, I'll gladly stay or come back."

"I need a bath now!" Marcus yelled. "I can't sleep in my own piss."

Thelma pursed her lips and shook her head at Latice. "No, don't worry about it. You go ahead and go home. I'll deal with him tomorrow. I'm going to bed."

Marcus began to protest by pulling on the handcuffs. "This is inhumane!" he yelled. "You bitches won't get away with this!"

"Maybe if you stopped calling us bitches, we'd treat you nicer."

Marcus's voice was a near growl. "You and that fat-assed police wannabe can kiss my ass."

Tired of his ranting, Latice retrieved the jar from her purse, opened it, and let one of the insects fall on Marcus. She watched him yell and scream. The author wiggled as best he could, but the bug only skittered across his body quicker. Marcus shook like a wet dog in snow.

It was in that moment Latice got her breakthrough.

"Okay! Okay!" Marcus screamed as tears flowed from his eyes. "I'm sorry for calling you bitches—just get it off me! Please get it off me!" Marcus broke all the way down and wailed out in fear.

Latice brushed the bug away and stepped on it. She noticed Thelma watching Marcus in silent awe. "Come on," she said. "Let's let this nigga cry in the dark."

Latice pulled Thelma out of the kitchen and flipped off the light.

THELMA COULDN'T SLEEP. She had Marcus on the brain, and it was causing her to toss and turn, so much so that Monroe had gone from the end of her bed, where he normally slept, to the floor.

"I'm sorry, fella," she said as she threw back the covers and turned on the bedside lamp. "I can't sleep."

It was after midnight. She lit a cigarette and walked down the hall. Soon Monroe was right there with her, guarding her from any danger even though she didn't fear the darkness of her own house.

The pissy odor from the kitchen had already reached the living room. The smell burned her nostrils, reminding her of a nursing home she once worked at. She remembered the entire place smelling like piss and plastic.

Marcus was awake when she flipped on the light.

"Who's there?" he asked curiously.

"Me." She sat and watched him.

The author didn't waste a minute. "What? You've come back to make me shit my boxers too?"

"No, I was actually coming to give you a bath."

She put the half-smoked stick out and stood over him. "If you kick me or try anything with these legs of yours, you better kill me, got it?" Her threat was real, and she knew Marcus had that much common sense.

"Where's the bucket and towel?"

"I'm taking you to the bathroom for a real bath."

"Are you going to take these handcuffs off me?"

"Is Minister Farrakhan married to a white girl?"

"Whatever. Just get me cleaned up," he replied. Marcus's tone was now flat and void of any sarcasm or contest.

Thelma assumed it to be his nice way of agreeing. Once she had his underwear off, she cuffed his ankles together and taped his knees securely, allowing her hands to make contact with his skin as she handled him. Marcus was warm-blooded. Again, his muscles gave her butterflies. She removed a key from her house robe and unlocked one of the handcuffs. Marcus allowed her to recuff his hands behind him once she unhinged the metal holders from around the pipes. She picked him up, straddled him over her shoulder, and carried him to her room, where she laid him on the bed.

He propped his legs up. "You got a nice bed. A king for a queen."

Monroe growled Marcus into silence.

Thelma set the temperature of the water and added some peppermint oil and gingerroot foaming wash, her own aromatherapy to kill the acidic stench of the urine.

She scooped him up and walked him to the tub, where she placed him in the rising suds.

It had been a long time since she'd had a man around, and even though Marcus wasn't much of one, he was one nonetheless, and quiet as it was kept, she was mildly attracted to him. It had been hard fighting it, but Thelma liked Marcus's bad boy intellect and his body.

As she watched him sitting in the tub, Thelma was reminded of what she missed, how beautiful a fit and trim brother looked in the raw—a human one, anyway. Raylene was possibly right. Monroe *was* great at protecting, but there were so many other things he couldn't do. The thought of betraying Gwena crossed her mind. This man had once played a game that ended in rape charges, and he was the cause for the dissension that nearly destroyed Second Pew, but Thelma couldn't deny that Marcus had energy, and his energy was speaking to the loneliness inside her.

"You smoke?" she asked. There was no shame in her question. Thelma believed in keeping it real at all times.

Marcus looked at her, like a slave being told he was free. He had to lean forward to keep from leaning back on his hands. His eyes wandered into hers. "Smoke what?"

She left Marcus to his thoughts while she took her time going for her secret stash. She already had a few joints prerolled. Thank God. Thelma grabbed one of the joints and went back into the bathroom.

When he saw the gift she was carrying, Marcus's head fell to his chest. "You make it hard for a brother to be mean." He looked at her and smiled. "Hell yeah, I smoke."

Thelma nodded and smirked. "You seem like the type." She watched Marcus settle into the water. "Sorry about the incident with Latice," she said. "I didn't know she was going to go that far."

"It's okay—this bath makes up for it."

"Marcus, why did you agree to play that game?"

Marcus thought. "I was young. That was the one thing in my life I wish I could take back."

Thelma continued lathering the soap in the towel. "Do you hate women?"

"No, but I'm not trying to settle down with them either."

"Then why call them bitches?"

"Thelma, not now."

"Why not now? Now is as good a time as any."

Marcus shrugged. "I just think women try to get over too much. Women whine and complain too much when it's the men out in the world busting their asses to make this world go round."

Thelma thought about his words. There was something underneath Marcus's voice that made him vulnerable to her. He had no problem opening up even though she'd lashed out the most cans of whip ass on him. "I would really like to see you write a book that is about real love for once instead of drama and negativity."

Marcus sucked his teeth. "Love doesn't sell books." He took a good look at her.

"Speak for yourself."

"Why are you being so nice to me all of a sudden?" Marcus asked with a true interest.

"I feel sorry for you."

"I don't need your pity, and I don't want to talk about the *incident,* if you don't mind."

Then Thelma confessed. "I also wanted to spend some time with you. I figured since you're here, I might as well take advantage of it."

"What is that supposed to mean?" Marcus looked up at her. His stare was curious but intense.

She tested the temperature of the water, got her feel on massaging his muscular legs. "It means that I might as well enjoy you while you're here." Thelma dried her hand and lit the joint. She puffed it to get it going and then placed it between Marcus's lips. She grabbed the medicated Vaseline that was under the sink and moisturized his lips.

"Thanks." He inhaled, closed his eyes, smiled. "You church girls never surprise me. The biggest undercover fr—"

"Don't say it." Thelma held up her hands. "Unless you want me to drown you in this tub."

He thought. "Well, you know."

"Men act like a woman can't be discreet about her sex life." She turned off the water. Marcus had bubbles up to his chest. She puffed, puffed, passed, and when it came back, she ashtrayed the joint. She took the towel and raised it to his shoulders. She watched him drift off each time the warm water flowed down his body.

"Fake is more like it. I've been with women who had dugouts that were like being at a class reunion. You're happy to be there, but it sure is a lot of niggas around, you know."

Thelma laughed. "Whatever. I think it's fine for a woman to be sexually uninhibited. Men are that way all the time."

"Waiting for pussy is like waiting for water at the river during a rainstorm."

Thelma felt the old Marcus coming back, but she didn't mind. She could handle him. "Then why do men marry?"

"They don't know any better. That's why I have to keep it real and hold it down for the fellas. I'm doing for men what Terry McMillan did for women. I give them a voice by writing fiction that doesn't put all the blame on the brothers." Marcus talked with conviction. "That's what I do."

"Come on. You're Marcus Brooks." She washed his back. "Surely you don't think it's that simple."

"It is that simple. There ain't a man alive who wouldn't hear this and not agree. He may not say it, but he damned sure believes it."

"I don't believe that." She let her eyes wander around the room. Giggled. "My grandparents were together for sixty-seven years."

"All that means is that your grandfather either found a woman he could control or he was codependent." Marcus smacked. Sucked his teeth.

"What?" She stopped washing, frowned, and looked at Marcus. "Are you talking about my granddaddy?" She swatted the soap-soaked towel at him, splashing him in the face playfully.

Marcus ducked. "No, never mind what I said." He let himself relax against the back of the tub, making sure he leaned over so he could be closer to her.

Thelma continued rinsing. "I knew you could act tame with the right temperature of water."

Marcus smiled. "Thanks for the bath. I appreciate it."

"You're welcome." She got up from the side and dried her hands. She hit the joint again, but this time she didn't pass it.

"What about me?" Marcus asked. "Puff, puff, pass, remember?"

"You miss a turn for talking about my granddaddy." Thelma smiled.

"Aren't we a little old for this?"

"Calling women bitches, talking about my granddaddy, or smoking weed?" Thelma asked. She covered her mouth in an attempt to hold in her giggles but couldn't contain herself.

Suddenly Marcus broke out in laughter as well.

Thelma reached in to get the towel. As she put her hand in the water, Marcus leaned over and planted a soft kiss on her lips. Thelma pulled back.

Marcus relaxed. "Don't act like you don't want it," he said. "I've been feeling your vibe, and I say we go ahead and do something about it."

Thelma blinked in openmouthed shock.

She allowed Marcus to lean back and land another soft kiss on her arm, making his way up to her shoulder. Thelma leaned in close. His kisses were nice.

When their lips met this time, she fought losing her cool. She had to remember that Marcus Brooks was the enemy in more ways than one. He represented everything she stood against when it came to defining a good man. She pulled back. "I can't."

Marcus jerked away from her. "Don't play."

Thelma mechanically wrung the towel and then put it away. "If I fall for you, I'll stand for anything."

"What?"

"I mean . . ." Thelma's brain must have stopped sending messages to her mouth, because she fell speechless. It was wrong being attracted to a bad boy like Marcus. Nothing good could ever come of it.

"Get me the hell out of here!" Marcus sneered under his breath, careful not to alert Monroe in the next room. "This is the kind of shit I'm talking about. Teases, all of you. Women who don't know what the hell they want!"

Monroe growled.

Thelma grabbed Marcus's mouth, squeezing his jaw between her thumb and fingers. "Nigga, it's called changing my mind. You don't have to get angry just because you're not getting what you want. Neither am I." Thelma flipped the tub stopper. The water began to flow out as she continued ranting. "I'm not some ho off the street, and you are not running anything around here. You got it?"

"Suck my—"

Whack!

A swift backhand from Thelma cut his sentence short. The force of her opened hand against his cheek shut him up. His head reeled back as a stunned look shadowed his face.

Marcus moved his mouth around. "I guess I deserved that."

Thelma grabbed a towel and lifted Marcus out of the tub. She took him to her bed and laid him out, being careful not to lay him too close to any possible weapons.

She grabbed a bottle of lotion from the dresser, squeezed a dollop into her hands, and began to lotion him. "Why do you carry that picture of your mother around with you?"

She caught Marcus's attention. "She died some years ago."

"Sorry to hear that."

"She was the only woman in my life that I could trust and depend on."

"Is that why you treat everyone else like shit?" Thelma massaged the moisturizer into his skin, careful to get the areas between his toes and the rough spots on his heels and ankles. "Or have you always been that way?"

"My mother was a beautiful woman who taught me about women and taught me how to be tough."

"When did women ever need you to be tough?" Thelma asked. Thelma helped Marcus to his feet.

"My mother had my back. She didn't let any girl ever get close to me."

"Sounds like she was a little overprotective and a little jealous."

"I can see that," Marcus admitted. "I was an only child, and my mother made sure every girl went through her before they got to me." He smiled. "I'm glad too, because most of the girls were tramps anyway."

"You know this for sure?"

"My mother told me."

Thelma fell silent. She searched Marcus's face for some clue that maybe he was kidding, but he wasn't. Thelma finished her work without another word. The silence between her and the author was thick enough to bump into. She put Marcus into a pair of her old pink-and-green college sweats.

"Tell me about your father." This time Marcus's question caught Thelma off guard.

She exhaled. "All I ever knew about my father was that his name was Jimmy Roy, he was from Texas, and he was a musician. He went out for cigarettes when I was six or seven, so I don't remember much." Then she stared at nothing in particular. "You know how that goes. If it wasn't for my mother, I wouldn't know what little I do know."

Marcus sighed. "You know more than I do. My old lady wouldn't tell me shit about my father. She hated him and never let me see my dad." He paused. "But then again, my old man never came looking for me either."

Thelma saw the emotion drain from his face as Marcus tried to laugh off his pain. She felt sorry for him. For a moment she wanted to set him free. He had enough marks against him already.

They heard Raylene's bedroom door open.

Thelma hurriedly sneaked Marcus back to the kitchen. She didn't want to get caught by Raylene, because if she did, she'd never hear the end of it.

RAYLENE LEAPED FROM HER BED when she heard Thelma leave her room, pass by, and go into the kitchen. She rushed from her room, sneaked quickly into Thelma's, and quickly surveyed her surroundings. She tapped her fingers on her teeth in thought. *Where is it? Where does Thelma keep her weed?* Raylene wasn't even sure she was still going to try it, but she was sure she needed to get it just in case she chose to go through with her plan to do the un-Raylene-able. After the drama with Marcus and the women, she needed more than two small pills to make her relax. She really hated him and was glad that Thelma didn't mind doing most of the caretaking. She hoped the weed didn't kill her. *In the bathroom? I don't have that kind of time. The dresser?* Raylene searched the dresser, quietly looking through the drawers.

Smoking wasn't new to her. She'd picked up a small smoking habit in high school, but that ended after her mother found out, which was two days later. When Wanda Nix discovered that Raylene was "trying to be grown" as she put it, she made her daughter smoke an entire pack. Made her sick for a week. She stopped smoking that day, but never forgot. *Not on or in the dresser. Where else? Closet?* Raylene ran over to the closet and searched Thelma's shoe boxes and shelves but found nothing. If she was going to call Greg Alston and ask if they could hook up tonight, she needed to be high to do it. She had grown courage over the last few hours, but not enough. She figured the Mary Jane would give her the push she needed. Thelma was always more loose when she was high, so what could this one time do? Not in the closet. *Under the bed! Hurry!* Raylene ran to the closed side of the room. Thelma wouldn't immediately see her if she came in. *Ah! The wooden box! Eureka!* The box was out of reach, on the far side from where she kneeled. Then, Raylene scooted halfway under the bed. Suddenly, she heard Thelma enter the room and slid completely under the bed.

Raylene heard voices. Thelma's and Marcus's. She hoped they couldn't hear her heartbeat against the hardwood floor.

Thelma's padded sock-covered feet moved around the bed frame and then disappeared into the bathroom. Water began to run. Raylene's eyes bucked. *What in the hell is going on? Under no circumstances is Marcus to be removed! That's the rule. Marcus is to be wiped clean and assisted from the floor in the kitchen. Those are the rules! Unless . . .* Raylene realized she wasn't the only one being naughty tonight.

Thelma's feet returned, shifted, and disappeared into the bathroom again. Carrying Marcus with her this time, she closed the door.

Raylene took a breath and peeled open the box. She grabbed one of the joints and made a quick and quiet exit back to her room.

❧

She held the joint in her hand and stared at the thing as if it were going to light and smoke itself. This lasted five minutes after she'd put a towel under the door, cracked her window, and lit a scented candle. Finally she looked up Greg's number. She was surprised that he was listed. She marked the page, put the book down, and grabbed the lighter.

Three puffs in and ten minutes later, Raylene was half-baked. She put out the doobie and grabbed the phone book. Dialing the number took another five minutes. . . .

"Hello?"

"Yes?" A woman's voice answered. She sounded sprightly and energized even though it was after midnight.

"I'm sorry for calling so late. Is Greg Alston available?"

"He is. May I ask who's calling?"

"Oh . . . Greg and I went to high school together. . . ." *What if this is his girlfriend or wife instead of his sister?* Raylene began to lie. Something she didn't think she was good at and avoided as much as possible. "I'm on the class reunion . . . committee and . . . was calling to see if he would be interested in serving on the food committee for the next event."

The distant screams of a baby in the background disturbed Raylene's high. The child sounded small, maybe two or three years old, but healthy. She was crying for her daddy. The woman shuffled, the child's cries subsided.

"Who's calling?" the woman asked again.

Calling Greg is a bad idea.

Raylene hung up. She wasn't a home wrecker, high or not. She was even mad at herself for going there. What she and Greg had in high school was over. Back then, she'd gotten a little buck wild too, but Raylene kept her business so personal that the only people who knew were her and the men she'd been with. Greg was the type who could keep a secret of the passion they brought out in each other. Just thinking about the intimate times they shared still aroused her if she put too much thought into it, like now.

She put the phone on the floor and turned out the light. She needed to go to bed. Fatigue draped her, but a hunger in the pit of her stomach pulled her from her room and into the kitchen.

Marcus wasn't on his pallet. But Raylene didn't care. She made a beeline for the fridge, grabbed a bowl of grapes, and took them back to her room.

She felt bad about calling Greg's house, but at the time it felt like the right thing to do. She and Greg always had an understanding that superseded boundaries until now. Now, he was married with children, not a boyfriend. Now, the face of the scene had changed. Raylene was a grown woman, and she realized she needed to find an adult relationship that was fair and just and honest.

She wondered if Greg still had that smooth way of taking a woman's panties off while licking the inside of her navel. Raylene fell slowly back in the bed and closed her eyes.

Greg Alston was the one man she remembered who could work it the way it needed to be worked.

Raylene slid her fingers into her panties. She closed her eyes and thought about Greg's soft kisses and the tender way he entered.

She felt wetness on her fingertips. Her warm juices flowed from her. As Raylene found her G-spot, she nestled into the pillows and raised her knees. It had been a while since she'd touched herself, and never had she touched herself in a sexual way. But the high was making it easy. She could almost feel and see Greg on top of her, his hands guiding her back across the bed for comfortable positioning. It was then that a wave of sexual wanting overcame her and she dived into herself, allowing her fingers to work for her and bring her to what Raylene figured had to be the big O, because a party like that had never gone on between her legs before. She shook against the pillows, biting her lips, coming down into her own bed of smiles.

Her thoughts wavered to Will and the wedding. The truth was she no longer trusted him. The truth was there were other things about Will Raylene didn't like, and the bad times with him already outweighed the good. He was warm but lacked passion. He was good looking and suave but lacked humility. He was thoughtful, but thought only of himself. Will was a package on the outside, but on the inside he was a mess, and Raylene knew that when she met him. She had to face it—she had her own issue of wanting to be married so much that she was willing to marry a man who lacked passion for her. It didn't get any plainer than that when God talked. Raylene snuggled into the covers and blew out the candles. She'd done the un-Raylene-able, and it had changed her life.

LATICE WAS AWAKENED by the phone. She sat up and removed her night mask. She glanced at the clock. It was five thirty in the morning. An uneasy feeling settled in her stomach. It had been this way since the kidnapping. Each time the phone rang, it was like a death toll demanding her to answer. She picked up.

"Latice?" The voice on the other end took her by surprise.

"Who else is it going to be? Rodrick, what do you want?" She had no patience for her ex-husband or his games.

"Did I wake you?"

Latice rolled her eyes and propped herself against the pillows. "Yes, you did. Lance is still sleep—you'll have to call him later."

"Actually, I need to talk to you about something that's been on my mind. It's serious."

"Something serious is on your mind, Rod? I can't believe it."

"Tice, I didn't call to fight."

"Then what did you call for?"

"I want Lance to come and live with me. I've already talked to him, and he wants to come."

A bolt of shock went through Latice followed by the ill feeling of betrayal. "Rod, how could you go behind my back and talk to Lance about something like this? He's still a minor, and I am still his legal guardian."

"He's grown enough to make his own decisions, and I would like to spend some time with my son before he goes off to school."

"Finally after all this time you want to be a father? Great," she snapped without raising her voice.

Latice was known for her calmness, which she attributed to her father and his entire side of the family, who lived by mottoes like *Do the right thing, Don't let anyone stop you from doing what you know is right,* and *Don't be surprised by the actions of others.* "Because," her father always said. "Niggas will always be niggas, and you must know the difference."

So, for a long time, Latice knew what Rodrick was about once he decided to walk out and never look back for fourteen years. He was about nothing. "No."

"He's almost eighteen. When are you going to let him go?"

"Why are you trying to hold on all of a sudden?"

"Tice, I don't want to fight."

"You've said that already, but your actions say different."

Suddenly seventeen and a half years raising Lance and watching him grow flashed by Latice. She remembered paying for her son's traffic tickets, buying his school clothes, giving him money for field trips, and cleaning up his vomit when he thought he was grown enough to stay out all night and drink with his buddies at fifteen. "Until he's eighteen, he will do as *I* say, and how dare your monkey ass call me at this hour in the morning trying to pull the wool over my eyes!"

"Then you'll have to tell him he can't come. Are you prepared to do that?"

"I've been prepared ever since your sorry ass walked out." Latice hung up.

Now unable to sleep, she got up and flipped on the television to catch the morning news. Marcus Brooks's headshot on the screen was the first thing she saw. Latice felt her face tighten. She moved to the edge of the bed and listened.

"I'm reporting live here in Dallas in front of the Gypsy Tea Room, where an anonymous tip led police yesterday. The person reported that Marcus Brooks was last seen here with a group of ladies proclaiming to be a book club and fans."

Latice grabbed the phone to call Thelma, but there was no dial tone.

"Hello?"

"Hello?"

"Latice, this is Naomi. I'm sorry for calling this early, but I need to talk."

"I was just about to call Thelma. Are you watching the news report?"

"No . . ." Naomi's voice trembled.

Latice muted the television when she realized Naomi was in tears. "Sweetie, what is it?"

"Vincent's gone, and I don't know what to do."

"What do you mean *gone?*"

"I think he's left me. Most of his clothes are gone, his shaver, his favorite CDs, pictures of the kids . . . all gone."

"Are you sure?"

"Yes. We had some words yesterday before I came over to the house. It was about the same thing it's always about."

Latice interrupted. Naomi had been confiding in her for over a month, complaining about how Vincent wasn't helping her.

Latice asked, "Did he leave a number?"

"No, just a note saying he'd call my mom's to talk to the boys."

Latice's mind swam as she tried to think of the best advice to offer. First of all, she was supportive of Naomi's marriage, which was her Christian responsibility. Vincent was a good guy, and if Naomi would learn to back up off him a little bit and stop being so picky, then maybe she would appreciate what she had. Secondly, Latice considered those babies, and it was important for kids to see their parents together. "You need to go over to your mama's right away and stay there until your husband calls. When he calls, listen to him."

"But I do listen to him."

She cut off Naomi's pending rebuttal. "Girlfriend, I've seen you around your husband, and I know you don't listen to him."

"Well, if he would do more positive things around the house, then I would, but children need stability, structure, and attention. Latice, you know I'm calling you because I know you know how I've been feeling lately. Vincent is not being very understanding to what's going on with me."

"And I sympathize with you, sweetie, but that don't mean you can't be wrong."

"Did I tell you he let the boys eat jelly beans for lunch last Tuesday? An entire bowl full of those nasty Harry Potter jelly beans and how cute he thought it was when they realized the candy gave them gas so they played some fart game?"

Latice laughed. "Are you kidding?" She thought it was cute too.

"I'm serious," Naomi whined. "I don't want our children thinking it's cute to do that in public."

"Maybe that's the problem, Nay. When it comes to your husband, your house, and those children, you're too busy trying to control it all. Is that what you want?"

"You're supposed to be on my side." Naomi gave a poor last-ditch effort at refusing to admit wrong.

"I am. You're obviously upset that Vincent is gone, and I'm telling you what I think you should do to get him back." Latice's alarm clock went off. It was six o'clock, time for her to get up. "You need to allow him to be and enjoy him when he's home. Stop being so convinced about how you think things should be, and just let them be sometimes."

"Thank you so much. I needed to hear that." Naomi released a sigh of relief. "I just hope he comes back home before Friday." Then Naomi asked Latice the one question she hadn't even thought about. "Do you think we're going to jail for kidnapping Marcus?"

Latice thought about the question. With as much as she knew about the law, she also knew that laws were made to be broken. But in real life, the criminals rarely if ever got away. "I don't think so." She rubbed her belly in an attempt to uncork the pack of butterflies that had nested there.

Naomi sighed. "Okay, I'll talk to you later." Disappointment laced her voice.

The doorbell rang. Now what? Latice looked out her bedroom window, which faced the front, and saw a police car in her driveway. The butterflies in her stomach began to spasm. It was already too late.

She pulled on her house robe and slid into her slippers as she reminded herself to keep her head about her. This could be unrelated to the kidnapping. Maybe some of the mutts in her neighborhood were being stolen. She hoped so. She said a small prayer that the police not be coming by to take her off to jail. Then she headed down the stairs.

When Latice opened the door, a male and female officer stood before her. "Is this the home of Lance Harris?"

"Yes, it is," she answered. "How can I help you?"

The female officer propped one leg on the porch. "I'm Officer Cobb, and this is Officer Sanchez. We're here to see Mr. Harris."

"For what?"

"Are you his mother?" Officer Cobb's voice was polite and nonthreatening.

Latice's eyes darted back and forth between the two.

"Ms. Harris, your son has been charged with an assault that reportedly happened Friday night."

"What do you mean he's been charged?"

"The victim is pressing charges. We need to take Lance in for questioning."

"What victim?" she asked. Lance's name had no business coming up in something like this.

"We can't say just yet," Officer Cobb said. "But the girl says she goes to the same church with Lance."

Latice turned around and faced the top of the stairs. "Lance!" She turned back to the police and invited them in.

Lance's bedroom door creaked open. "Yeah?"

"Get down here." She stepped up into her kitchen, where she could still be seen from upstairs.

Lance came trotting down the stairs, half dressed in pajama bottoms and no shirt. When he saw the police, he slowed his pace. His face grew pensive, making him look like the cat that had eaten the canary.

Latice caught the look. She noticed her son's nervousness, fear, and guilt.

"Son, this is Officer Cobb and Officer Sanchez. They have some questions to ask you." She took a lean against the doorjamb. "Sit down."

Lance plopped himself down in the leather recliner. "What's up?"

"Do you know Christy Ellis, son?" Office Sanchez took a seat on the couch across from Lance.

"Yes, I know her."

Hearing Christy's name made Latice's legs weak. She walked over to a nearby rocking chair and sat down.

Officer Cobb cleared her throat. "Lance, were you with Christy Ellis on Friday night?"

Lance sat back, cocked his legs open. He was being bold, looking like his father and pissing Latice off with his attitude. "Yeah, I was with her."

"Did you get into a fight with her?"

"Yes." Lance looked around innocently. "She got mad at me for calling her a whore, and she hit me, so I hit her back."

Latice massaged her temples to ease the rising outrage. Christy Ellis was the sweetest and most respectable girl at the church. She was smart, talented, and had been accepted to Sarah Lawrence.

"Lance, why would you call her out of her name?" Latice asked.

"Mom, I know you probably won't believe me, but Christy is a freak. She was all over me at the movie theater, and I wasn't feeling it. I did like you told me and tried to talk to her, but she got mad and tried to fight me. When I told her the truth about herself, she slapped me, so I hit her back and left her at the theater. I called Dad, and he came and got me and brought me home."

Officer Cobb cleared her throat. "So you admit to hitting her?"

Lance shook his head. "Yes, but she tried to force herself into my pants, and I wouldn't let her. That's why we got into it—I swear it's the truth." Lance sucked his teeth. "That bitch don't have a case against me. She hit me first. It was self-defense." Lance crossed his hands over his chest. "And besides, I still have her lipstick around my—"

"That's enough, Lance!" Latice said. She was beyond mortified with her son. "Have you lost your everlasting mind?"

"Don't worry, Mama." Lance sucked his teeth again. "I can handle myself," he said. "I got this."

"Lance, I didn't raise you to be the fool you're being right now."

Lance got up. "I'm a man now. I can take responsibility for my actions, because I didn't do anything wrong."

Lance's tone jarred Latice. "Son, you don't seem to understand. These officers are here to take you down to the jail. This is serious."

"For what?" the boy asked. "I didn't do anything."

Office Sanchez said, "You admit to hitting the woman?"

Lance shook his head. "It was self-defense, but yeah, I hit her."

"Foolishly putting yourself into the system," she said. Latice was suddenly unattached and unattracted to the boy who carried her contagious smile, thick hair, and walnut skin.

The officers handcuffed Lance. The boy began to beg and plead for Latice to save him as she had so many times before. His begging used to work, but she didn't know him right now, and maybe protecting him all these years had been a hindrance instead of a help.

"But, Mom, I didn't do anything!" Lance didn't struggle. *He at least knows better than to struggle.*

"Maybe a trip down to the detaining center will teach you how to put that ego of yours in perspective, instead of thinking that being a man means putting your hands on women. Lance, I warned you, and now there's nothing I can do but bail you out."

"It was self-defense!" Lance said. "I'm telling the truth."

"I know, son," Latice said. "And the truth shall set you free."

Latice didn't even take the time to watch her son be escorted to the blue-and-white car. She was mad, hurt, afraid, and unconcerned all at once, and so much more. She'd lost her motherly control, and Lance was allowing himself to be swallowed whole by the world before he could even liberate himself from the house, and Latice was tired of fighting for him. She was also angry that all her fighting didn't seem to add up to a hill of beans when it came to Lance making decisions for himself.

She picked up the phone and dialed the number for Rodrick that was saved on the caller ID. When he answered, she subdued her anger.

"I've changed my mind. You can take Lance."

Rodrick didn't immediately respond.

"What? You didn't think I'd let him go?" She huffed. "We gotta start somewhere, right?"

"Right." His tone was dry and uninterested. "When can I come pick him up?"

Her lips began to quiver. She felt like she was betraying Lance. Turning him over to the wolves was something she never thought she had to do, but he was spoiled, arrogant, and believed the world revolved around him when it didn't. He needed to be with his father.

"You can pick him up at Lew Sterrett. You'll need to call a bail bondsman because Lance is in police custody and he will probably be detained."

"What is he doing in jail?"

Now he's interested.

Latice hung up the phone and turned off the ringer and went upstairs to her room. She would not be going to work today, and the anonymous tip to the police regarding Marcus no longer intimidated her. It was time to get off the roller coaster she'd talked herself and her friends into getting on. The past few days' events had finally taken their toll.

MARCUS OPENED HIS EYES to the silence of the house. Sunlight filtered through the kitchen, giving it and everything in it a golden glow. It felt like autumn even though it was midsummer.

"Hello?" he called out, wondering why the quiet troubled him. *Surely, I haven't gotten used to the sounds of the women's voices and the growls and barks of that stupid dog.*

Nothing mattered more than the fact that he had to piss.

"Thelma! . . . Raylene! . . . Gwena! Are any of you bitches in there?

"Excuse me, but I need to go to the bathroom!" He called out but got nothing. The sound of a motor broke the silence. Thelma's garage was connected to her kitchen, and if anything was going on out there, Marcus could hear it. It was the garage door. Someone was coming home.

The door opened. Thelma entered wearing nothing but a thin cotton clutch that looked more like a kimono. Marcus noticed she was drenched from head to toe.

"Is that sweat or water?" he asked.

"I'm wet," she said before removing the light jacket. The unveiling revealed her wearing nothing but a G-string and matching lace bra set. The russet color of the lingerie gave Thelma's skin a soft, almost dreamy appearance. Victoria was about to tell Marcus her Secret.

Marcus smiled. "Now that's what I'm talking about. If you're going to hold a brother hostage, at least make it worth his while." He wiggled his toes and bit his bottom lip. "I knew you felt something for me."

Thelma put her hands to her lips. "Shhh. They might hear us." She walked over to him and seductively climbed on top of him. "I've been wanting you since you got here."

Marcus licked his lips. "Right. I hear you, baby. Keep talking." He could feel his nature rising as she removed his handcuffs, allowing him to sit up so he could look into her eyes.

Thelma was finer up close and half-naked. She was big in all the right areas, thick like Marcus preferred his women.

He put his hands around her and flipped her over onto the pallet. "I finally got you where I want you," he said as he leaned down and began kissing her on the neck and tasting her skin with his tongue. "Damn, baby, you are so fine. I feel like I've just been released from prison."

Her laugh was a shy one as she opened her legs, allowing him to pull off the G-string. She'd applied some shimmery stuff around her legs, giving her entrance a glittery look. Marcus felt like he'd arrived at the red carpet of sexual pleasure. She'd gone all out for him, and he appreciated it. With two fingers, Marcus checked Thelma's lotus as he continued kissing and running his tongue across her skin, angling down to her lips and then down to her nipples. A warm river of readiness flowed between her legs, and Marcus was ready to swim.

"I think I love you," Marcus heard himself say. "You're strong, opinionated, fucking gorgeous, sexy, and you listen to me. All that could make a brother like myself want to change. I could marry a woman like you." Marcus nestled his face between Thelma's breasts. She arched herself into him. He looked up at the ceiling. "Lord, I'm about to wax this ass," he said.

He guided himself inside her with slow and careful attention. Once he was inside and found a rhythm with her, an overwhelming sense of joy came over him, and he began to cry. "I'm whipped," he wailed.

Thelma's voice wavered in his ears. "Ever have a ménage à trois?"

Marcus pulled back. The thought excited him, and expectation blanketed his face. He looked around the room. "Who is it? Gwena? Raylene? Naomi? Hell, I'd even take Latice. Fat women need dick too. I'm down!"

"Naw, motherfucker!" Suddenly a six-foot-three, solidly built, naked black man stormed into the kitchen like chocolate thunder.

Marcus felt his heartbeat take a break. "Aw, shit!" he heard himself say in a tone two octaves above his own.

The man's chest muscles jumped as he stormed over, and picked up Marcus and threw him across the floor. Pain shot through Marcus's body, and his heart went from zero to infinity in less than three seconds.

Knowing he was no match for the intruder, Marcus tried to talk some sense into the giant man. "Look, man, if this is about Thelma, I'm sorry, but look at how fine she is. You have a fine woman. Okay, go ahead and kick my ass."

"That's not what I have in mind," the man said. "I'm not naked for nothing. I'm trois."

Marcus whimpered under his breath. "Man, I'm sorry, but I don't get down like that. I'm a *heterosexual* black man."

The man slapped Marcus on the ass. "Shut that shit up!"

Marcus jumped. "Ok-k-kay, dude. T-t-tell you what. I got money. Why don't you help me get out of here, and I'll pay you some money. Whatever you want. When my next book comes out, I'll pay you. How does two hundred fifty grand sound?"

"Nigga, your next book ain't coming out!" the man said.

The intruder grabbed Marcus, manhandling him like a puppet, and bent him over on all fours on the mattress and held him there, daring Marcus to try and escape. Then, he began rubbing Marcus's ass with gentle merry-go-round strokes.

"Please!" Marcus shot back, begging. His heart was beating with such fervor that Marcus had to clutch his chest. "*Bitches* is as good as done. I may even get a movie deal."

"I said it ain't getting done! You will not release *that* book!" The man slapped Marcus on the butt. The sting cut into Marcus's gut. Marcus hollered. "Okay, it ain't gettin' done!"

"And the next time you call a woman a bitch, you better think twice!"

"Okay, okay!" Marcus pleaded.

He could feel the man standing behind him, making him suffer as he waited for what was about to happen. A sudden rush of adrenaline invaded Marcus's being, and he found the courage to do the unthinkable.

Marcus attempted to fight back. He closed his eyes and began to kick, hoping to land a foot to the large man's abdomen, but the thrust of his foot felt like he was kicking into oatmeal, which only made Marcus kick harder. So much so that he woke up kicking and swinging as best as the handcuffs would allow him. Frantically, he peered about wild eyed, trying to remember where he was. When he realized he was dressed, alone, and safe, Marcus relaxed until he looked down and saw that his crotch was surrounded by a patch of wetness. His face grew hot. The dream was a sign that he had to stay alert. These women were crazy, Thelma included. Hell, she was probably the one who meant him the most harm. He had to get free.

He studied the pipes beneath the sink as he'd done so many times before. The darkness consoled him, but this time it also revealed something else. It was something that gave Marcus hope, and he wondered why he hadn't seen it before. There, above his head, set to the right of the piping was a small, jagged corner of metal, sharp enough to be a weapon. Marcus maneuvered the rusted cuffs over the edge and began rubbing the metal against metal. After a few minutes, he checked. There in the rust was a clean mark of friction. It was going to take some concentrated effort, but if he remained focused, he would be free, possibly by nightfall. Marcus got to work.

Gwena walked into the television station, drinking her Starbucks, feeling like she was on cloud nine. She no longer had worries of the Marcus Brooks kind. *Acuna matata.* The book club had let her walk away with no arguments. They also knew she wouldn't say anything.

Starvette Gilliam spotted Gwena and ran up to her.

"Girl, have you heard the drama that's going on?"

"What drama?"

"The anonymous tip about Marcus Brooks. They suspect he's been taken by a book club. It's been on the news all morning."

Gwena concealed her concern by sipping the caramel macchiato. "Really?"

"Yes, but guess what?"

"What?"

"We've been out doing a camera poll, and most of the people who've been following the story think it's great!"

Gwena forced herself to smile. She didn't want to seem too obviously concerned. "What about the tip?"

Starvette shrugged. "It was anonymous—that's all I know."

As they walked through the corridor of cubicles, the slow stench of garbage ebbed from the area. Gwena knew the smell.

"Oh, I forgot to tell you," Starvette whispered. "There's some old transient woman waiting for you. She's been here for about two hours waiting. That's what you smell."

The odor became too much for the talkative camera hand. She touched Gwena before leaving. "I'll talk to you later, girl." Starvette hurried away, looking like she was trying to hold her lunch down. There she left Gwena alone to ponder who was in her cube. Her curiosity ceased when she saw Jonnie Coleman.

The woman jumped up and ran over, getting into Gwena's face. "There you is! I've been wondering when you were going to be here."

Gwena put her things down and protected her nose with her hand. She stared at the woman, took in the soiled jeans, tattered Budweiser T-shirt, and Birkenstocks covering feet so ashy, they looked like they'd been used for mashing flour.

"I was just about to start walking around." The woman's bloodshot eyes searched Gwena's. "Remember me? Jonnie? Jonnie Coleman?"

"I remember. You're the thief."

"I never take what ain't due me anyway. And if you call me a thief again, I'm going to the police. Forget giving you the chance to help a broke sister out. I ain't no thief. I'm a hustler, honey."

"My apologies then." Gwena propped herself on the flat of her desk. "What can I do for you?"

"I want the only thing that's important." Jonnie tapped the desktop. "Money."

"Excuse me?" Gwena took offense. "Ms. Coleman, I don't know what you're talking about."

Jonnie pointed a thin finger at her. "I know you and your friends have him. The author. Marcus Brooks."

"Ms. Coleman, I resent—"

"Stop right there," Jonnie commanded. "See, what you don't know is that after I ran off that night, I doubled back. Something told me to come back to see if that man was going to be okay, because you hit him pretty hard and nobody seemed concerned with calling the police."

Gwena took a deep breath and released it. "I see."

"I saw everything."

"Are you the one that tipped off the police?"

Jonnie flashed a dirty-toothed grin. "At first I wasn't going to do it, but I had to get your attention."

Gwena attempted to reason with the woman. "If it weren't for me and my friends, Jonnie, you'd probably be dead. We saved your life."

"But I ain't dead," Jonnie boasted. "I'm alive, I'm broke, and I need the money, so I'm not trying to hear how grateful I should be."

"So how much do you want?"

Jonnie sat. "I want five thousand dollars. Each of you give me a grand, and I'll be on my merry way."

"We don't have that kind of money."

"You mean to tell me a camera operator, a dog doctor, a hair-stylist, interior designer, and a goddamned security officer can't come up with five grand? Now, I know you hos ain't that broke."

"What if we don't want to agree to your terms?"

"Then I call the police, tell them what I know. I'll tell them I saw you hit Marcus and then put him in Thelma's car and took him to Morning View street in Highland Hills. Right now, they don't know that. They just know he met up with five women."

"How did you get Thelma's address?"

"I'm a hustler, baby." Jonnie smiled. "Don't ask a hustler about hustler business."

Gwena knew the situation was serious. "I'll check with them," Gwena said. "How much time are you giving us?"

Jonnie looked at the crystal desk clock next to Gwena. "Until eight o'clock."

"I don't get off until six," Gwena said. "My bank closes at five."

"That's not my problem, Miss Cotton Candy Curls," Jonnie said. "Have my money by eight, or I go to the police and tell everything." Then she added. "And I won't make it sound like no mistake."

"How do we get in touch with you?"

"I'll call you back at five o'clock sharp and tell you where to meet me. That'll give you enough time to get on the horn and gather up my green. And don't try no funny stuff."

"Ms. Coleman, can't we at least get an additional hour? You're cutting it a little close."

"You better watch how you talk to me, honey." Jonnie spat the words from her lips as she pointed a thin, ashy finger at Gwena. "I don't take nice to disrespect. Now you either agree to eight or you go to jail before five."

"Fine," Gwena finally said. "Eight o'clock."

Jonnie got up and skittered out. Gwena wanted to grab her and somehow shut her down, but Jonnie was too funky to even touch. She didn't even bother to chase Jonnie down the aisle.

Slowly, Gwena sat down in her desk chair, picked up the phone and began calling the club members one by one. The ladies agreed to meet for lunch so they could decide what to do.

Elaine's was packed as usual. No matter what day it was, the small Jamaican restaurant stayed overflowing with customers. When Gwena arrived, the others were already seated, waiting for her.

Latice looked like she hadn't slept in days, and Gwena carried a look of despair that read defeat. Only Raylene, she noticed, sat composed and optimistic.

Latice and Naomi seemed the most haunted by inner pain; the circles under their eyes were evidence of missed sleep.

Gwena slid into the empty seat at the table.

Thelma was the first to say it: "So what are we going to do?" She didn't like the idea of being blackmailed by a woman who didn't have sense enough to bathe. Frustration was in her tone.

With the exception of Raylene, the others were downcast. Naomi's face was scarlet, and her eyes were puffy from crying.

"I say we turn ourselves in," Latice suggested. "This has gone too far already."

Gwena watched her friend. Latice's head was not in the game anymore. She could see that Latice was worried about her son.

"How's Lance?"

"He's still at Lew Sterrett. His father is supposed to get him out. I'm waiting for him to call me." She rubbed her eyes. "I say we let Marcus go and just turn ourselves in. That will kill this entire blackmail attempt."

"I don't think we should quit," Raylene said. "We've come too far."

Latice rolled her eyes. "We can't keep Marcus forever, and getting him to change has all but backfired. Besides, Jonnie Coleman shouldn't benefit from our attempt at doing something right. I don't care. Our intentions were and still are good."

"Tice is right," Naomi added. "Besides, I don't want to go to jail."

"None of us do."

The waitress came over and took everyone's orders. Once she was away from the table, the conversation picked back up.

Gwena rubbed her hands through her hair. "Look, why don't I just turn myself in. I have a suitable motive, and I'm sure it's what Marcus wants anyway, to see me behind bars."

"No," Raylene intervened. "We're not going to let you take the fall for something we all agreed to."

Thelma joined in. "She's right. We're not going to be cowards about this, no matter what we decide."

Naomi began to cry at the table.

Gwena leaned over and comforted her. They were falling apart, but she refused to believe they were out of options. Raylene had the right idea. Women all over were cheering for them, and it wasn't time to quit even though all the signs might say so.

It was the first time that no one had anything to say.

The waitress delivered the food, but the women only picked at their plates.

"Okay, enough of the sad faces," Raylene said. "Let's put our heads together. We can beat this."

Thelma talked through a mouthful of curry chicken. "What are you thinking?"

"I don't know, but surely if we got away with taking Marcus, we can get away with giving him back without getting caught. Book clubs are rooting for us."

Latice shook her head. "We're not the Five Musketeers, Ray. I don't give a damn if the world is cheering for us—in a court of law, cheers mean nothing."

"I think we should hear Raylene out," Thelma said to Latice. "We heard you out, so let's give her a chance."

Latice grew upset. "Our personal lives are suffering because of this."

"You should have thought about that when you were struck with the grand idea to kidnap the most impossible man on the planet," Thelma snapped. "Now I think we should exhaust all of our options before we go turning ourselves in. I'm not ready to go to jail no more than anyone else at this table."

"Thelma has a point," Gwena added. "No offense, Latice, but we should at least think about what can be done."

"Fine," Latice said. "But whatever we come up with, it better be good."

Naomi had time to call Vincent. She'd already moved everything to the backyard for the taping of the confession and was
now waiting on Thelma, Latice, and Gwena to return with Jonnie
Coleman.

She stepped in the kitchen and grabbed the phone off the wall.

Marcus was on the floor, twiddling his feet. "I have to pee," he
demanded.

Naomi looked down at him while she dialed the number.
"Give me a second—I have to make a call."

"Look, I'll let you handcuff my hands, just let me go to the
bathroom. I can't hold it."

"I said, *wait!*" She dialed the number and waited for an
answer.

"Hello?"

"Vincent." Naomi found herself at a loss for words. "Hi."

She heard him take a breath. He sounded busy. "I'm in
rehearsal—what is it?"

"I was calling to talk."

"About?"

"*Us.* I want you to come home."

"I thought I wasn't good enough for us."

"Vincent, please just hear me out," Naomi said. "I *know* you're
a good father. I *know* you're a good husband. I'm even sorry for
thinking that your watching Marcus Brooks was a serious matter

to you." Naomi nervously curled the phone cord up in her fingers. "Honey, I want to talk. I want to tell you how sorry I am for taking you for granted. I miss you, and I just want things to be cool between us. I love you more than anything."

"Oh, please!" Marcus hollered so loud from under the sink, his voice echoed.

"Who is that?" Vincent asked.

"Baby," Naomi said nervously. "I have something to tell you."

"He doesn't know your dirty little secret?" Marcus said. "No wonder he left you!"

"Baby, is that another man?"

"Yes," Naomi said. She sat at the table after she gave Marcus a swift kick to the ribs. He bowled over in pain.

"Naomi?"

"Vince, you remember the other night when you mentioned that the police were looking for Marcus Brooks?"

"The author?" Vincent paused. "Yeah, I remember."

"Well . . ." Naomi wasn't sure if she should say anything, so she bit her lip instead.

"Your bitch-ass wife is holding me hostage!" Marcus answered for her.

"Naomi, is that Marcus Brooks?" Vincent asked.

Naomi quickly tried to explain "Yes, but I promise you, baby, that we're turning ourselves in at ten o'clock tonight."

"What in the hell were you thinking?" Vincent said. "Look, I'm coming to get you. Where are you?"

"Thelma's." Naomi began to cry. "Vincent, I'm sorry, baby, and all those things I said about your dad and your parenting, I take back."

"It's okay." She heard her husband laugh. "I'll be right there, and we'll get you out of this fix together."

"I love you." Naomi hung up the phone and wiped her eyes.

"He's weak," Marcus said. "Your husband is as weak as Eric Benet at a nympho party."

"No, you're the one that's weak," Naomi said. "You wouldn't

know the first thing about having a woman call and beg you to take her back."

"I got plenty of women begging to be with me."

"But are they begging to stay?"

"I don't want them to. I'm a bachelor, and bachelors know better than to let a woman lay claim to his shit."

"Whatever," Naomi huffed. She was sick of Marcus's mouth. "You never have anything good to say."

"Why should I?" Marcus intoned. "I'm being held hostage." He gritted his teeth and then squirmed on the floor.

Naomi watched Marcus wet his boxers.

"I told your bitch ass I had to piss!"

Naomi narrowed her eyes. She was outraged at Marcus's immaturity. "Just for that, you can wait." She grabbed a small can of paint from a cabinet and opened it. It was blue, the color they had planned to use on the podium. "You'll have to wait until the others get back."

"Isn't Raylene here?"

"Yes, but she's busy getting things ready for Ms. Coleman."

"Who?"

"The woman you gave the two dollars to."

"What is *she* doing here?"

"She's blackmailing us."

"And you're letting her?"

"Of course." Naomi didn't see the harm in spilling the beans now. Operation He Had It Coming was about to close down for good. Everything was in place, and by ten o'clock, this would be a fading memory. "She threatened to go to the police if we didn't pay her five grand, so we offered her something better."

"Better like what?"

"Better like going on local television and making a plea for our pardon. She's going to make a statement."

"That's bullshit!" Marcus said. "You need to go to jail for what you've done to me!"

When Naomi walked by, she felt Marcus's foot slip under her.

She spilled paint on him and fell to the floor. When she saw Marcus's hands come from around the pipes, she became horrified. Her feet felt like they had melted into concrete cinder blocks. Naomi opened her mouth to scream, but Marcus was quick. He had his hand over her mouth before the breath could leave her throat. "You say one word, and I'm going to snap your pretty little neck. You got it?" Marcus leaned over her like a black moon. He grabbed the tape from the drawer and made Naomi lie on the mattress. As he taped her mouth closed and roped her ankles together, she lay panic-stricken.

Raylene's voice called out to her from the front. The front door was open, and voices filled the house.

Marcus put his finger up to his lips, gesturing for Naomi to keep quiet, and for her own life's sake, she did. As Marcus listened to the voices, Naomi prayed that when Vincent came to get her they would all still be alive.

Jonnie stood on the corner of Ross and Washington, waiting for an emerald green BMW to pull up. Gwena said they would be there at seven thirty sharp, but Jonnie didn't have on a watch. She left her house at a quarter of eight and assumed it to be about that time. As she looked up and down the busy street, she didn't recognize the remote television van that rolled up to her. It wasn't until the door opened that she noticed.

Gwena was seated in the front passenger seat. She patted the paper bag. "We have your money. Get in."

"Let me see the money first," Jonnie said. She was being careful not to get hustled. The last time she was anxious during a hustle, she got a paper bag full of dog turds instead of the cash and ended up having her phone and electricity turned off. Gwena held the sack open so she could get a glimpse of the fresh green hundred-dollar bills.

Latice invited her inside the van.

Jonnie took a last look up both ends of the sidewalk and jumped in. Once the van door was closed and they were on the street, she began to ask questions. "What is this about?"

"It's about justice," Gwena said. "We have a proposition for you that could double your money."

"Keep talking about money." Jonnie liked to talk about making money, and she'd done it all from selling stolen goods to selling herself for a little cash. However, she was tired and desired to just be able to have enough money so she could move out of the city. She was tired of the fast living. She was tired of Dallas.

"We want to put the cameras on you."

"For what?" Jonnie's eyes searched for reason. "I'm not one of America's most wanted, am I?"

"Nothing like that," Latice said. "We want you to tape your confession of what happened that night. Clear our names."

Gwena handed Jonnie the money. "Consider that a down payment. We'll give you the rest *after* the tape is done."

Jonnie liked what she was hearing. "I can do that." Jonnie shook her head. When it was all said and done, she'd use some of the money to get her teeth fixed, and the rest she'd use to go back to her hometown of Calvert, a quieter, more subdued part of Texas. She had family there. Jonnie looked around.

"What's the paint for?"

"We'll tell you when we get to where we're going," Latice said. "For now, just sit back and enjoy the ride."

Jonnie puffed up her chest. She was important now. These women needed her.

"How am I going to enjoy a ride when I don't know where I'm going? For all I know y'all could be taking me to the police to make this tape. I already told you that I don't mess with no police."

"We're not taking you to the police. You're going somewhere better."

Jonnie thought for a moment. "Well . . . I guess anyplace is better than the police department." She laughed. "Except Lew Sterrett." Panic hit her again. "Y'all ain't taking me to the jail, is you?"

"No," Thelma said. "We're taking you to Marcus."

"Oh, no," Jonnie said. "Stop this van. I want to take my money and go on about my business. I'm not trying to get all caught up in this mess." She tried to get up, but Latice removed a gun from her holster and handed it to Gwena.

"What's the gun for?" Jonnie asked.

"Insurance." Gwena's order was edged with tension. "Now sit."

"Come on, we ain't gotta pull out the lead," Jonnie begged. "Look, I'll even leave the money—just don't make me face that monster again." She tossed the bag over. It landed just shy of Latice's feet. "Please."

"Too late," Latice said. "You started it. You finish it. Then, you get the rest of your money."

Jonnie touched her chest. "Why me?"

"Why not you?" Thelma said. "If it weren't for you, we wouldn't be in this foolish predicament."

Jonnie sat back without saying a word. She was in a pickle and had no idea how to get out of it. She could jump from the truck at the next light. The only thing was that they were on the freeway, and even if they weren't, she knew she couldn't move fast enough for at least two of the three women. Gwena and Thelma both had on outfits that would let them run.

"I can't win for losing," she said to herself.

"Neither can we." Latice kept the gun aimed. "Do you know that before we met you, we'd just come from having the time of our lives?"

"Oh, yeah?" Jonnie asked.

"That's right," Gwena added. "We'd come from a concert, and all we wanted to do was get home. But we stopped to save your ass, and now it's time for you to save ours."

"Save y'all?" Jonnie said. "Shit, I can barely save myself."

"Whatever," Thelma said. The van slowed as it exited the freeway.

Jonnie knew where she was. Highland Hills. They were going to Thelma's house.

"All we want you to do, Jonnie, is make a statement that we saved your life that night and after that you ran off."

"All right," Jonnie said, "I got it. Can I get a close-up?"

"Sure," Gwena said with a modest grin. "Anything you want."

"I've never been on television before," Jonnie said as she patted her hair and tried to fix her clothes.

"Then get ready because this might just make you famous."

Famous? Jonnie let the thought go to her head as any thoughts of being rich always did. She saw herself hanging out with Diana Ross, Samuel Jackson, and Sidney Poitier, her three favorite entertainers. And she could finally make her move on Denzel Washington. Surely Gwena had to be telling the truth, because the equipment in the truck was something fancy.

"I can't be on television looking like this," Jonnie said.

"We have that taken care of," Latice said. "Just ride. We're almost there."

And so Jonnie picked up the bag of money and held it close. She sat back and got lost in her own thoughts again. In her gut she felt that these women, guns and all, were something special, because they were picking and paying her to pull a hustle. The great thing about it was Jonnie considered herself the number-one hustler in Dallas. Probably in the world.

When they pulled up to the house, Jonnie clutched the bag of money to her chest and jumped out. "I'm ready!" she said. "Ready for the rest of my money."

"First you take a shower and then do the video before you get it. Got it?" Thelma asked.

Jonnie shook her head. She was ready for her fifteen minutes of fame. No longer caring about Marcus Brooks and the threat he posed, Jonnie followed Gwena, Thelma, and Latice into the house.

Thelma had a nice place. It reminded Jonnie of the bottom of a genie bottle. Silk pillows on the couch, fine linens covering the windows, fancy doodads and whatnots, including expensive picture frames. Jonnie felt like she'd hit the jackpot.

MARCUS HAD TO FIND HIS THINGS. If he were lucky, he'd be able to get out of the house without seeing any of the women, but he had to move quick. He didn't want to hurt any of them, but after his fight with Thelma, he knew he would if he had to. And God forbid he'd have to kill the dog.

Several voices came from the living room. They were all in there. He grabbed a knife from the kitchen and tiptoed through the den. His heart pumped wildly in his chest.

"I'm going to check on things in the kitchen." It was Gwena, and she was coming in his direction.

Marcus pressed his back to the wall, and before Gwena could feel him on her, he cupped his hand over her mouth, grabbed one of her arms and folded it behind her, snatched her body into his, and whispered in her ear. "If you try to get away, I'm going to snap your arm in two and then go for your neck—you understand, bitch?"

The breath from her nose was rapid against his fingers. Gwena nodded. She smelled like nectar, sweat, and shampoo. Marcus walked her to the kitchen, tied her down, and taped her to one of the chairs. Marcus smiled when he saw the gun nestled inside her pants.

He removed it and examined it carefully. It was a nine millimeter. "Were you planning on using this on me?"

She shook her head.

Marcus whacked her with a swift and solid backhand. "Yes, you were. Don't lie to me."

Gwena couldn't take the blow. She was crying before Marcus could hit her again, which he did. Gwena fell limp in his hands.

Monroe began barking from the garage and scratching on the door. Marcus jumped up. The commotion was eventually going to bring another one of the women his way. He looked in the dryer and grabbed two bedsheets. He covered Naomi up and disappeared into the house with the gun. Now, he had leverage.

❧

Thelma's house was nice. Marcus could tell she had taste as he whizzed from the kitchen to the den again. She liked the same colors he did: browns, greens, oranges, reds. Autumn colors. When he peeked around the corner from where Gwena came, the coast was clear, but the front door was open. He wondered if they had all gone back outside. Voices came from the bathroom. Marcus took another peek. It was Raylene, closing the door carefully and retreating into her room. A slit of light peeked from under the bathroom door across the hall. Someone was in there taking a shower.

Marcus skimmed down the hall past her room to the last door. As he passed the mirrors lined along the hall, he captured a glimpse of himself. He looked like a freak show. The blue paint, bandages, soiled clothes; he looked a fool. He recognized Thelma's room right away. His clothes were neatly folded on a nearby chair. Marcus grabbed them and ran into the bathroom. As swiftly as he could, he got undressed, hoping he wasn't wasting too much time, but it was important to him to look halfway decent so that when he went to the police, he wouldn't look like James Brown did the last time he went to jail.

The sound of whistling came into the room. Marcus grabbed

the gun, held it close, and stepped behind the bathroom door. He assumed it to be Thelma, but hoped it was Raylene. He wasn't ready to settle his score with Thelma just yet. She'd been the biggest cause of his fury, and he wanted to make sure that when he got his hands on her she'd never forget it.

The sound of footsteps couldn't be heard, because of the carpet in the bedroom, and Marcus had to strain to hear the intruder. He grew anxious. Monroe's barking from the garage had become high pitched and full of warning. He had to get out of the house before that mutt was let in. He stepped from behind the door and charged out of the bathroom.

Raylene never saw him coming. He thumped her across the head with the butt of the gun and watched her fall to the floor unconscious. She'd be out for a while. Three down—he wasn't sure how many to go.

The sound of the front door closing left him no time to go back into the bathroom. He grabbed Raylene's arm and drug her to the far side of the room and left her beside the bed, out of sight. He stepped into a bedroom doorway when his eyes picked up on the shadow coming his way.

"Raylene, are you back here? I need you to show me how to work this video camera." Latice's voice held no caution or alarm.

She would be another one he was going to have to hit over the head, but he could also use her as collateral. Monroe still barked. Marcus darted out into the hall and used the butt of the gun to stun Latice, and then he grabbed her. She dropped the camera.

Marcus wrapped his arm around her neck and talked gently to her. "Go to the kitchen," he said.

Latice wobbled in his arms, and he could tell she might have a concussion. Blood trickled from her scalp. "How does it feel to have your life out of your control?" he asked.

She remained silent.

Sheets still covered the other two; however, Gwena had managed to maneuver over toward the door leading to the garage. She was trying to let the dog in. Marcus hit Latice again, knocking her out completely. Then he ran over to Gwena and pulled her away from the door. Her voice was only muffled whimpers from behind the tape. Her face was beet red and flooded with tears. Her eyes looked at him with a numbed horror. Marcus aimed the gun at her temple. "Try it again, and I'm putting a bullet in your brain."

Her head fell submissively.

"Yeah, look at the shit you've caused!" Marcus said.

"What in the hell is going on?"

He turned around, and there she was. Thelma had walked in unaware of what was going on until it was too late. Marcus put the gun on her. "Make one false move, and I will kill Gwena."

Thelma's arms flew into the air, surrendering.

Sweat was now dripping from his paint-covered body.

"Marcus, you don't want to do this," Thelma said.

"Try me and see."

She raised her foot to take a step.

"Don't move."

Thelma put her foot down. "Why don't you just go. Latice could be dying." She looked around. "Where's Raylene?"

Marcus laughed. "In the back, trying not to go into the light." He was enjoying taking no prisoners. These women had done him dirty, and retribution was feeling way better than total freedom right now.

"We treated you nice—why don't you do the same?"

"Nice!" he snapped. "You call tying me up to the sink nice? If that's nice, then what I'm doing now must be worthy of a Nobel Peace Prize."

"Marcus, we figured you would change. Rewriting that book would make a lot of women happy."

"Fuck y'all! What have women ever done for me but brought me misery?"

Thelma took a breath. "See, that's your problem. Your mother is dead. Let her go."

"Bitch, don't talk about my mama."

"She's the root of your problem. What grown man sleeps with

a picture of his mama beside his bed. Women don't do that kind of shit, so why would a man?"

"Bitch, shut up." Marcus felt like a boy. The only other person who'd ever teased him about that was his best friend, James Acey, but that was years ago—still, Marcus felt twelve again.

"That kiss we shared last night—that was the Marcus I know. Your mother didn't want you to have love in your life. Don't you get it? She was miserable because your father walked out on her, and she wanted you to be miserable too!"

"Thelma, I'm not going to tell you again."

Junesta only ever wanted what was best for him—he knew that. That's why she didn't allow him to date. She cared about him; that's why she asked him questions and gave her opinions about things. She was a loving, caring mother. Marcus's chest began to quake. Tears blurred his eyes. Junesta's words resonated in his ears.

"Marcus, son, I'm the only bitch in the world who really, really loves you. I carried you for nine months right here." She touched her belly, *"I know what you like to eat, I know what you're allergic to, and I know what your dick looks like."*

"Aw, come on, Ma," Marcus said, embarrassed. He hated it when his mother drank and "got real" as he called it. *"Don't you have any shame?"*

"Not when it comes to my son."

❧

Marcus's body quaked with impending tears.

Thelma took a step in. "Marcus, you have to forget your mother and stop being so angry."

Marcus cocked the gun against Gwena's chest. "I said don't move!"

Thelma stopped.

Marcus stood there, naked, crying, confused; the gun was aimed and ready to go. From the corner of his eye, he saw another person standing quietly in the shadows with a video camera. The woman holding it was in ancient-looking clothes that didn't quite fit. She looked familiar as she held the camera away from her face and smiled at Marcus.

"When I sell this tape to the news people, I'm going to make a fortune!" There she was. The woman with his two dollars. She was holding a video camera, the red light still blinking. Marcus felt a shard of anger rip up through him like lightning to a tree. She was the reason! The woman flinched when she saw Marcus's stare harden into her own frosty browns. She licked her tongue out at him and then at Thelma before dashing out of view.

"Son of a bitch!" Marcus shouted. He pointed the gun toward the wall and began shooting at the old woman. He took the shortcut through the den, hoping he'd get to the front door before she did. Marcus was too slow, but he was close enough to give chase. That tape could destroy his career. His bare feet burned against the concrete, but with a little more effort he could catch her.

He aimed again and pulled the trigger with as clear a shot as he could pull off. The old woman zigzagged back and forth, gaining momentum. The odd thing was, she was still able to catch him on tape. But no matter how fast he ran, Marcus couldn't catch up.

The running had him tired. Marcus fell to his knees where he stood and put the gun to his head. It had come to this. He'd fallen from grace, and at the bottom of his throne was a videotape with him on it. And on this tape he's seen knocking a woman out with the butt of a gun. He's seen crying. He's seen being dealt with. Worst of all, he's seen butt-naked running down the middle of the street shooting a gun. He was finished. The echoes of a dog in the distance announced the arrival of two police cars. Marcus closed his eyes and yelled. "Don't come any closer or I'll shoot myself, I swear!"

Then he saw it. The real news camera that was getting it all right now. Marcus couldn't win for losing. He squinted to get a closer look, and to his dismay, read the letters CNN. His fall from grace had just gone national. Marcus tightened his index finger on the trigger.

REGIS WAS LOOKING FOR MARCUS. He'd called every number he had, but only got sent to voicemail. Only an hour ago, he'd gotten off the phone with Stephanie Dillon. She wanted to reconsider the option. *Bitches* was such a hot topic right now, she saw where she could benefit despite the fact that Marcus was an ass.

He'd held out stalling for the author as long as he could, but Marcus was nowhere to be found, and the cocky son of a bitch wasn't returning any of his calls. He didn't mind Marcus playing spoiled and stubborn, but when it came to losing money, that was a different story. Now he was pissed. Wherever Marcus was, Regis hoped he was having a bad time.

His Lower East Side Manhattan flat was like a diamond in the rough. It was located just fifteen walking minutes from his job, and the seven-hundred-square-foot studio was only twelve hundred a month. The interior was part brick wall, part regular Sheetrock painted an amber color that gave the room a club feel by day and a lounge feel by night. However, around him were walls so thin that he could hear his neighbors' television. Bridgette and Gary lived next door. They were watching CNN, and apparently something on there was very funny because they erupted in laughter.

Suddenly there was a knock on the wall. "Hey, Regis, you need to see this," Gary called out. "Put your tube on CNN."

Regis turned on his television, never responding verbally to Gary. The communicating was fine, but sometimes they got on his nerves. Bridgette was one of those women who loved to sing but couldn't, and Gary was the one who couldn't stay quiet during sex. He always sounded as if he were next door alone.

As he flipped through the channels, he thought about his big meeting tomorrow with Faulkner Lorraine. She was a best-selling author trying to make an exodus from her current agent and looking for a new one. Regis needed the work. She was being heralded as the next big name in contemporary fiction. If he could get her, it would more than make up for his Marcus Brooks loss.

When he flipped to CNN, there was his former client, naked, in the middle of the street, with a gun to his head. From out of nowhere, a dog jumped into the picture and knocked the gun out of Marcus's hand. Then police swarmed him and took him into custody. Regis's mouth fell open. Marcus looked like he'd been to hell's hell and back.

Bridgette's and Gary's laughter exploded from the other side of the wall again, and this time Regis couldn't help himself. As funny as it was, he knew Marcus had probably gotten into some serious trouble behind this one. As an agent, he'd known Marcus's transgressions with women and carried the burden of knowing he'd helped protect the author when he'd known his client was wrong.

Regis refused to help Marcus out of this one, even if he did beg. Whatever the story behind the footage, he didn't want to know. The bottom line was that it was funny as hell, and knowing Marcus, the man had brought it on himself. At least now, he knew where in the hell Marcus Brooks had been.

Marcus Brooks was the laughingstock of the publishing world. He couldn't turn on the television or radio without hearing people talk about him.

To make matters worse, he had legal woes. He was facing all kinds of charges. From assault and battery to possession of a firearm; even the kidnapping was now a farce because of the news coverage.

His life was over. He'd been locked in his apartment for days without reaching out to anyone. His answering machine was full with messages from magazines like *People, Esquire, GQ, Savant,* and *Essence* wanting the exclusive scoop on the story behind the video. They finally wanted him, but no amount of money right now could make him talk about his experience. It was too humiliating.

He wouldn't rest until he got revenge on each one of the women, which he planned to do as soon as he patched things up with Regis. He'd fire his agent after Regis did some damage control to keep his career from hitting rock bottom.

Today was as good a day as any to ask his former agent's forgiveness. Regis answered on the first ring.

"Regis, my man!" Marcus faked a smile through the phone. "I'm back . . . back from Dallas."

"So I've seen," his agent shot back. "Nice shot of you running around the streets of Dallas high and naked. Man, what were you thinking?" Regis's tone was challenging and solidly unforgiving. He didn't like being that way and found it uncomfortable even when he did get angry with people he considered to be his friends. Marcus was one of those people. Regis's tone flattened. "I'm listening. I don't have all day."

"I need your help. My career . . . I need to get back on my feet, Regis. I know you have connections."

"What about the times I've needed your help, Marcus? You have single-handedly almost ruined my career with your selfishness, and there's only so much I'm willing to do."

"Can I at least explain?"

"Sure, man. Be my guest."

"These bitches tortured me first of all by—"

"Will you stop calling women bitches!" Regis yelled into the phone. "You think I want to keep dealing with that?"

"Look, man. I'm just trying to tell you what happened to me, and I'm not going to change my language just because you don't like it. I was kidnapped by some bitches. That's the truth."

"Peace, Marcus."

And like that, Regis was gone. He'd hung up, leaving Marcus stunned and frustrated, holding the phone.

He placed the receiver back on its base and threw the phone across the room. Marcus grabbed his mother's photo and threw it against the wall. "You ruined my life!" Then he kicked the wall as he thought about Latice, Thelma, Gwena, Raylene, and the crackhead. "You bitches!" he yelled at the walls. He swept his dresser with his forearm, sending its contents crashing to the floor. "You haven't heard the last of me!" he yelled to the ceiling. Then Marcus fell on his bed and became a sobbing mess of angry flowing tears.

Dear Journal,

I'm out of the hospital and recuperating at Thelma's. I'll be here at least until I can move around a little faster, which will be another month or two. My head is still tender from where I was hit with the gun, but the stitches are out and the swelling has gone from grapefruit to plum. Everyone made it out of the incident alive, and I'm thankful for that. Last night we all sat around comparing bumps and bruises, talking about Marcus and the fact that he offered to drop his charges in exchange for Eva Rubio dropping hers. She was glad to do it, once she found out Gwena was one of the infamous Second Pew Book Club members that was responsible for kidnapping and taking down Marcus Brooks. It all worked out, even though Marcus left Dallas unchanged and even angrier than before. It is my prayer that he somehow finds peace with his hostilities toward women. The entire experience gave me a courage I didn't have before, and it has made my life easier.

Will called to see how I was doing. We had a long talk about us, finally. I told him it was over, that because I no longer trusted him, I could not move forward with a wedding. Of course, he started quoting the Bible and begging, but I couldn't help him. Besides, there's a rumor floating around Mt. Z that Felicia Henderson is pregnant with his child, which I wouldn't doubt. I'm transferring my membership as soon as I'm better.

Maybe I'll join a small church on the outskirts of town with no more than twenty members. That would suit me fine. As soon as I get my own place, I will date again. Naomi wants to hook me up with Vincent's brother. His name is Sterling and he's an investment banker. I don't know about the name, but as long as he's not a preacher, then I'm game. I hope he likes to run. I'm very interested but in no rush to tie him down or be tied down. Naomi and Vincent are vacationing in Nassau on a second honeymoon. I've always envied her relationship with Vincent, but now I cherish and celebrate it. I now know that no man is perfect, but some are more perfect than others, and Nay has a good man.

I think Latice has had the hardest journey through all of this. Lance lost his scholarships, and the night that all hell broke loose he was sitting in jail, waiting for his father to bail him out, but we found out that Rodrick never showed up, never called. Nothing. Lance ended up being in there longer than expected because Latice was in the hospital. When she got him out, they were hit with the news that Lance lost his advanced intern credits and all of his scholarships except one. He's now a freshman at Howard University. The upside is that now Tice is working out every day, and so far she's managed to misplace twenty pounds at the gym. She looks good. Her goal is to fit into a 10, but I think she'll be an Oprah-sized 8 by the time she peaks.

Gwena calls me every day to see how I am. She's the only one who seems unchanged by everything. I still wonder about her. She has so many secrets I believe that have yet to be disclosed. The information about her and Marcus was news to me, and I still sometimes find myself trying to picture her and Marcus violently making love. All in all, Gwena is a true friend. It's really because of her that we're still together and can sit around now laughing about guns, kidnapping, and blackmail. She is our glue.

Nobody knows what happened to Jonnie Coleman. She took

the initial bag of money and ran. I'm assuming she pawned my minicam, but it's no big deal. The sacrifice was worth our freedom. Hopefully, she was able to use the money to stay off the streets. I hope so.

Thelma went out and bought another dog. She actually purchased a female companion for Monroe. She's a chocolate Lab named Lucy. The day Thelma brought her home, Monroe voluntarily stopped sleeping at the foot of Thelma's bed. Thelma says her feelings aren't hurt, but I can tell she sometimes misses the way things were. Her logic to buying Lucy was that just because she wasn't bumping uglies with anyone, Monroe shouldn't have to be denied the right to mate and do what was natural. Maybe now Thelma will put a man in her bed to take Monroe's place. I never told her what I saw and heard that night while under her bed, trying to steal a joint. First, I'm too embarrassed, and second, that was her moment. Whatever she and Marcus shared will be left between them, but I could see their attraction the night they had the fight. Who would have known? It's hard for me to fathom my best friend falling for someone as unsympathetic, self-serving, and vulgar as Marcus Brooks, but then again truth is oftentimes stranger than fiction.

MARCUS SAT IN THE OFFICE with Regis. After some groveling and a few trips to New York, he was finally back on Regis's client list and trying to return to the top of the bestseller charts. His latest book had been out for over two months, and Marcus wasn't happy with the reviews or sales. He tossed a copy of his latest masterpiece on the desk.

"I did what you told me to do. I changed the book, and now my shit ain't selling!" Marcus jumped from the seat, holding the book in his hand. "What in the hell happened to my marketing?"

Regis crossed his fingers in front of him. "Marcus, you're in somewhat of a funny situation," he said. "A hole you dug, if I may."

"May this!" Marcus started to give Regis the finger, but then halted. He'd already been warned by the agent that the disrespect would not be tolerated, and since no other agent would sign him with a ten-foot pole, Marcus kept his cool. He took a deep breath to calm himself as he returned his hand to his lap. "I'm a changed man, and this book is just as good as any that I've put out. As a matter of fact, it's better. It's about love."

"That may be so, but last year you pissed off a lot of women, and quite frankly, brothers don't want to be seen reading a book titled *Love Slave* written by a man of your caliber."

"Are they trying to say I'm gay?"

"They're trying to say that Marcus Brooks has changed, and

they're not interested in that. It's going to take time to reel in the women, but once you do, everything'll be fine."

Marcus sat back down. "I thought the fact that I refused to press charges was supposed to *reinstate my female readers!* What happened with that?"

Regis shrugged. "Things don't always go as planned." He held his hands up. "But, Marcus, have no fear. I've got you booked for the African-American cruise in November with seven other authors and seventy book clubs. That's a start. I'm certain *Love Slave* will be the talk of the trip. You'll outdo the others."

"I can't go on a cruise!" Marcus took the book and tossed it across the room. "I suffer from seasickness! My career is over!" The book landed on its spine against the wall, and he stormed from the office.

Regis picked up the copy of *Love Slave*. The book really wasn't so bad, but getting readers to pick it up had become a challenge. Marcus Brooks was yesterday's news, but Regis had faith that one day his author would bounce back with a vengeance. He wouldn't have it any other way.

Regis leafed through the pages. Marcus didn't do any acknowledgments this time; he only did a dedication. Regis looked at the name. *For Thelma Wade.*

He recognized the name from the newspapers and had even seen the woman's picture, but Marcus never talked about her or that week he spent under the sink at her house in Dallas. But Regis knew something had happened, because Marcus dethroned his mother from the dedication page and had given it to Thelma. He also no longer carried that picture of Junesta around with him. Whatever Ms. Wade had done, it changed Marcus. Regis let his imagination wander a few seconds before closing the book. *In due time, Marcus will make a comeback,* he thought with a hopeful smile. Regis placed the copy of *Love Slave* on his desk, sat back, and stared out the window, eighteen stories over Manhattan. *Yes, in due time.*